THE DARKEST NIGHT

THE SECOND DARK AGES

MICHAEL ANDERLE

DEDICATION

From Michael

To Family, Friends and
Those Who Love
To Read.
May We All Enjoy Grace
To Live The Life We Are
Called.

The Darkest Night
The Second Dark Ages 02

Beta Editor / Readers
Bree Buras (Aussie Awesomeness)
Tom Dickerson (The man)
Sf Forbes (oh yeah!)
Dorene Johnson (US Navy (Ret) & DD)
Dorothy Lloyd (Teach you to ask...Teacher!)
Diane Velasquez (Chinchilla lady & DD)

JIT Beta Readers
John Findlay
Micky Cocker
James Caplan
Joshua Ahles
Keith Verret
Kimberly Boyer
Jed Moulton
Kelly ODonnell

Thomas Ogden
Alex Wilson
Sherry Foster
Paul Westman
John Raisor
Mike Pendergrass
Brent Bakken

If I missed anyone, please let me know!

Editors
Stephen Russell
Lynn Stiegler
Ellen Campbell

LMBPN Publishing
PMB 196, 2540 South Maryland Pkwy
Las Vegas, NV 89109

First US edition, 2017
Version 2.00 (Edited by Ellen Campbell) August, 2017

FRANKFURT, GERMANY, APPROXIMATELY ONE HUNDRED FIFTY-
One Years After the WWDE

THE STREETS of Frankfurt were wet; the air was heavy and humid this dark night. Between the occasional sheets of rain coming down and her son asking questions, Sarah Bearnstred wasn't paying nearly enough attention when she took a left down the wrong alley.

"Oh!" She pulled little Michael close when she noticed the man farther down the dark alley turn around, holding what looked like a body close to him.

"What is it, Momma?" Michael asked, peeking around his mother's hip to stare into the darkness.

"Yes, what is it, Mother?" the man's voice asked from the darkness. Sarah was screaming inside, the aggravation she was feeling a moment ago lost in the recesses of a mind now paralyzed with fear.

"I'm sorry, I was trying to get back home." Sarah spoke in a clipped fashion as she took a step back, gently pushing her son behind her.

"I do believe," the man said as his footsteps clicked on the pavement in the alley, "that you are far away from home, little woman." He took another two steps into the pitiful light cast by a dim bulb that must have been salvaged from a building in the part of the city that had fallen into disuse. "I smell France on you."

"*Oui*," Sarah replied, as she took another step back. Now little Michael was almost out of the alley and Sarah set her shoulders. She was completely aware of who, no, *what* she had found.

And probably who, as well. "You are the Duke, are you not?" she asked, trying to keep as much fear out of her voice as she could.

The man paused and raised an eyebrow in surprise. "You know of me?"

"*Oui*," she agreed. "I've heard of you." She grabbed her young son's arm again, his curious nature not a benefit at the moment as he edged forward to see better. She pushed him back behind her once more.

"How delightful," the smooth voice responded as he took another step toward her.

Sarah kept her eyes on the man, who was now maybe ten steps down the alley. She had already accepted that her trip to this city was a mistake. She set her lips and knelt, pulling Michael closer. When he was next to her, she leaned over and kissed him on his cheek. "Momma loves you. Now do as I tell you and run down the street to our hotel. I'll be along to meet you at the room later."

"But..." the young boy started to argue, but stopped when his mother's fingers tapped his lips.

"Go!" she told him and was relieved when he obeyed, his running steps taking his little body away from the alley.

The man's eyes widened in surprise. "You are a brave one,

child. I can hear your heart," he said, taking another step forward. "Bah-bump, bah-bump, bah-bump." He smiled. "It is courageous of you to surrender your blood in lieu of your son's life. I am not a totally cruel and heartless man. I recognize the love you have for him, and I will honor the sacrifice you make."

"I won't go down without fighting!" she hissed. "You are the spawn of Satan himself, and..."

His rush caught her by surprise. Her feeble attempts to pull his head away, to separate from the teeth penetrating her neck, were futile. Sarah wanted to scream, but the languor that set in as he drew the blood from her body made that impossible. A single tear left her eye and traveled down her face. She had lost the ability to stand, but her body was held up easily by the man embracing her as he pulled her deeper into the dark alley.

Her final thoughts were of her son, hoping he stayed away and that the monster draining her blood would honor his word.

New York City-State

THE CITY WAS A DAMNED MESS.

Akio's ship hovered ten feet over the tallest building in the city. Through the night's cloud cover, he dropped out of the Pod and landed on the roof. He spent a little time looking over the city before making his way down to street level. He pushed out a bit of fear to keep the area around him clear.

He read the minds of those he encountered as he walked the streets. The most interesting bits of information came from the police.

There had been a major battle here that he and Yuko had helped fight just in the last day, and it had changed people in various ways. Some of them grew closer, some farther apart.

A few had killed themselves.

The fighting in this city was intense, and if it were any other time, he would stay and help. However, his duty, his obligation was to finding Michael and he was close.

He could feel it.

Akio allowed his mind and body to wander over to the airport, where he was able to read the men and women drinking coffee and talking while they worked. They were directing the various ships that had arrived before the massive battle to clamp onto the colossal towers, reeling them in and connecting them for passengers to debark.

Only one ship was currently connected to the immense structures.

One woman spoke to her friend as they came around the corner of a building. "We've lost them. The captain of the *Arch-Angel* said he was going into the storm to shake the pirates behind him." The lights behind them hid their faces in shadow as Akio read their thoughts.

He pursed his lips and melted back into the darkness. "Eve?"

"Here," the AI's voice came back.

"Bring the ship to me," Akio said.

"There is a hidden square about—" Eve started, but Akio interrupted.

"Here," Akio told the AI. "Now."

Sherry Logstrum let her friend continue to the control center as she stopped to enjoy the night for a moment. She pulled out a small stick that had been soaked in a few mildly soporific chemicals and placed it between her lips.

It helped keep the dreams away at night.

She happened to notice a man in a black robe with a hood over his head and a sword step out of a dark spot some fifteen paces away. He walked into the same area where the big fight against those creatures had happened a while back.

Sherry had taken a couple of steps out of the light to try to see better when the figure looked up. Sherry followed his gaze and her mouth dropped open when something as dark as the night floated down without lights. "You…" she whispered as the man opened the floating ship's canopy and jumped in. He turned in her direction and smiled. She could see his white teeth reflecting light.

"No, Sherry," the man said. "I am not a figment of your imagination."

With that, the canopy closed and the ship rose silently into the night. Sherry watched the sky, wondering if she would see it cross the stars.

Her stick lay on the ground, forgotten.

OVER THE ATLANTIC OCEAN, in the Renamed Antigrav Ship *ArchAngel*

MILES O'BANION, Captain of the ArchAngel was standing on the deck looking at the dark clouds that stretched across the horizon and the sea raging far beneath them. They warned him to turn either to the north or to the south.

If only he could. He looked over his shoulder and chewed on a toothpick as he eyed the ship chasing them.

He was tempted to raise the flag of the boat's previous owner, but he feared what the ship's present master would do if he found out more than he feared the results of the storm.

And he would find out, because one of the two youths—who were awake at the moment—would tell him. Especially the young and pretty one coming towards him right now. He sighed, answering this one was always challenging. Her mind was like a trap, fast and hard.

"Why aren't we turning?" she asked him and then followed his eyes. "Them?"

"Aye," the captain agreed. Short answers usually worked best with Jacqueline. She wasn't altogether human, but her curiosity was exactly like his wife's.

Jacqueline walked closer to the stern of the ship. "There are a bunch of people looking at us. I can't tell if they're all men or not."

The captain took a couple of steps to his right and spit over the side of the ship before returning to stand near the young woman. "Unlikely to be an all-male crew. There are many times that evil runs in the hearts of women, as well."

Jacqueline turned back to regard the captain. "Pirates?" He nodded and she pointed behind her towards the other ship, "Then why the hell aren't we waking up Michael?"

The captain chewed on the toothpick, biting harder as he jerked a thumb back over his shoulder at the dark storm clouds on the horizon. "Perhaps you can explain to me how anyone can sleep like the *dead* with that about to hit us? Even I can hear the deep rumble of the thunder, it's like he… Oh!" The captain's eyes widened, showing Jacqueline a touch of fear. "I meant no disrespect when saying he slept like the dead."

Jacqueline waved a hand at him. "I didn't hear anything." She mused, "I wouldn't suggest saying that around him, but I don't care. I grew up in a different generation." She looked at the captain and asked, "Why *aren't* we waking up Michael?"

He blew out a deep breath. "Because I would rather face the storm in front of us than the Master's temper should I wake him from a sleep when he specifically said to not interrupt him."

"And those guys?" Jacqueline asked, nodding towards the supposed pirates behind them.

"Rarely do they go into the storms; it can be too dangerous for them. So we jump into the storm just deep enough to get away, then choose another direction to cut back out. Worst that happens is the pirates pick the same direction we do and we meet up again outside of the storm."

"What about them coming into the storm with us, wouldn't that be the worst case?"

The captain nodded sharply at Jacqueline as he stepped towards the bridge. "Yes, and let's hope that doesn't happen."

THE PIRATE SHIP *FOLLY*

"MY NAME ISN'T BILLY the Bold because I shy away from a bit of rain!" the captain of the *Folly* asserted to his people. Those who didn't need to be on station had congregated on the deck as the captain pointed ahead of them. "There goes a fat sheep, and it's been far too long since *Folly* last tasted mutton!"

One of his ship's crew shouted out, "I thought you were called Billy the Bold because you asked Henrick's wife to screw you right in front of Henrick 'imself!"

Billy chuckled along with the general laughter of the crew. "My erstwhile best friend didn't give me a good description for Henrick. So yes," Billy winked at them, "that story is true as well." He twirled his hand and pointed again to the ship ahead of them. "But let's not lose the point I was making. We have a chance today to grab us a sheep who's thinking the storm will protect it from the wolves of the *Folly*!"

The same voice bellowed back, "I'm tired of stale bread and water, and I wouldn't be surprised if that fat fuck over there has real meat on board. Who's ready to eat some?" There was cheering at that.

Billy took the crowd back from his shipmate. "Then let's make way. Tighten everything up and let's be about it, you dogs." Billy looked over his shoulder. "The *Folly* is going hunting in the deep dark tonight!"

2

ANTIGRAV SHIP *ARCHANGEL*

"ALL I WANTED," Michael grumbled under his breath to himself, trying to keep the ire in his mind from being released through his now grinding teeth, "was a little peace and quiet to consider my next fucking steps."

He thought a moment about the curse word tripping off his tongue before his lip curled, remembering the red-eyed woman. "I'll be back soon, Bethany Anne."

He rose from the bed to take a couple of steps towards the door. The light, hesitant tapping from the captain was quieter than the thudding of the captain's heart. Michael could easily hear both through the thickness of the cabin door.

"Right after I kill a few more people who desperately need it," he concluded before turning the knob. He pulled it open.

Michael was looking down at the captain, who had a small drop of sweat glistening on his forehead, when a strong female arm shoved the nervous man out of the doorway and Jacqueline made her appearance. "Jacqueline," Michael nodded at her presence. "Using others as a shield, maybe?"

"No, *Sensei*, but the captain," she jerked her head in his direction, "thought he was man enough to knock on the door. But we both know if his heart beats much faster just because he needs to talk with you, he'll drop dead—" A loud *thunk* sounded beside her, and she looked down.

The captain had fainted.

She turned back to Michael and raised an eyebrow. He smiled. "I didn't say anything."

She rolled her eyes and put two fingers in the air, wiggling them next to her head. "You sure you didn't do some Vampire voodoo on him?"

Michael leaned into the hallway. Jacqueline moved aside so he could peer around the corner at the comatose captain. He straightened up and said, "Why would I do that?"

"Because you're Michael and shit." She pointed at the captain. "That right there is just your style."

Michael pursed his lips. "Okay, that's a fair accusation. But I didn't do it. He hyperventilated after you accused him of being too scared to talk with me and down he went."

"So, it's *my* fault?" she asked.

"Yes."

Jacqueline made a face and went to the captain. She bent down and picked him up, then looked both ways down the hall. His head made a solid *thwack* sound when she didn't pay attention while turning around.

Michael grimaced for the poor man as Jacqueline's eyes widened over her mistake. She adjusted the captain and lifted him over her shoulder. "I can't believe I have to go throw water on his face to wake his ass up."

"Keep hitting his head on the walls," Michael replied, "and it will take more than some water."

"He's not getting a kiss from this princess," she retorted as she took off down the hall. "By the way, *Sensei*," she yelled back, "we have pirates tracking our ship into a big-ass storm."

"Worse than that," Michael answered as he turned around. He didn't bother to raise his voice for the werewolf. "We have no captain at the moment.

THE PIRATE SHIP *FOLLY*

"MOVE YOUR LAND-LOVING LARDASS!" Billy yelled at two of the crew who were stowing a bit of the external equipment as the rain and wind buffeted them.

He pressed himself against the bulkhead to let them pass before taking opening the hatch to the bridge. He walked over to the controls and looked at the screen that showed all ships in the area. "Is that shit working?" he asked, leaning down to study it one more time. "It keeps fading in and out."

Electronics operator Sally David replied after glancing at the display, "'Bout as good as we can expect with the lightning and charged particles in the air, Billy." She reached up to grab a metal tool that she delicately tapped above the screen.

It cleared up.

Billy straightened up and rubbed his chin. "So, not too far." Just then everyone in the bridge reached out to hold on as the ship rolled to their left.

"*Sonofabitch*!" Mellon cursed behind Billy, who turned in time to see the young recruit slide the last five feet into a wall. Billy flinched at the sound of the collision. "Do a better job holding your ass up, Mellon!" Billy snapped before turning back to the screen. He looked through the starboard window, attempting to find an open space to allow him to see through the storm. Flashes of lightning lit up the clouds and the ship in front of them.

"I'm ready to eat some damned meat. Tell the crew down in

engineering and batteries we'll move the product and our new slaves over here, then gut that ship. We'll take all the tech they have. But that means we have to go faster, so redline those gauges! Let's come in like Hell's own demons."

"Aye aye, Captain," Sally David answered before turning back to her controls. She reached for the communications device.

Antigrav Ship *ArchAngel*

"What the hell!" The captain sputtered as he spit the liquid that was drowning him out of his mouth. He used his forearm to wipe the water from his eyes.

He blinked a moment, then looked into the grave eyes of the young woman staring back at him. "What happened?" he asked as he reached up to feel along his neck.

"Don't flatter yourself." Jacqueline smiled. "Michael isn't going to suck on your neck."

"Wasn't him I was worried about," the captain grumped as he accepted a towel to dry his face and what he could of his hair and shirt. He gestured at his body. "Got to make sure you didn't want a piece of this, then my wife would see a hickey and I'd be dead for sure."

Jacqueline smirked. "Now, that *is* flattering yourself. But it's also funny." She snapped her fingers to get his attention. "Hopefully, you don't have a concussion."

He reached up to touch his head, jerking his hand back when he encountered the sensitive area. "The hell!" He flinched again after a second try. "What happened?"

"You know, that's a story for another time," Jacqueline replied. "Let's play catch-up really quick." She started, but then the ship dipped, the power flickered, and the captain looked around, memory dawning on his face.

He reached out to grab his dresser to help himself to stand. "Why are we in here? *Gott Verdammt*, we're in a fucking storm!" He staggered to his door, his balance getting better the longer he moved. Jacqueline walked with him to catch him if he fell.

"Fainted," Jacqueline told him.

The captain stopped with his hand on the knob and looked over at the woman. "Aye, I do remember that part. What say we both agree not to mention anything about this last thirty minutes and I'll owe you one?"

Jacqueline took a second before holding out her hand. "Agreed, and let's go save our hides."

The captain opened the door, then shook her hand once. "Deal."

Back in his room, Michael smiled.

That girl was luck personified sometimes.

The bridge crew was fighting the storm hard when the door opened. Captain Miles O'Banion saw his first mate's relief as he entered the bridge. "Where are they?" he asked as he looked over the instruments.

"About half a mile aft and a little to port. Thought we might have lost them, but then they found us again and changed direction. We caught a bad bit of wind, and here we are."

The first mate's eyes flicked behind the captain and then back. His eyes returned to stare behind the captain, so Miles turned around. He saw the outline of someone walking down the hallway behind the frosted glass, heading outside.

"Don't ask," the captain ordered before anyone said something. "That's Michael. He'll handle our pirate problem."

Jacqueline harrumphed from beside him, "Taking all the fun, too. That grumpy-assed old man."

Miles turned to her. "He can't take you? How is he planning on getting there?"

"That's for him to explain and it's wouldn't, not couldn't," she replied.

"Why not?" Miles asked, his curiosity getting the better of him.

"Said he was annoyed at being woken up, so he needed to make sure he had enough targets to get it out of his system. I'd just get my bloodlust up and then he'd have less of his own fun."

"You know," the captain mused, "your family is seven different kinds of strange."

Jacqueline thought about herself and Mark and Michael and smiled. "I'll accept that as a compliment, Captain."

The captain looked around. "Where's Mark?"

The officer at the instruments looked over, a flush on her face. "Yes, where is he?"

Jacqueline wasn't sure if she wanted to punch the woman or roll her eyes. "He's outside making sure no one jumps on the ship while Michael is absent."

"That's dangerous!" she said.

She chose to roll her eyes. "He's fine, just bored probably."

THE PIRATE SHIP *FOLLY*

THE SEVEN PEOPLE were illuminated by the lightning coming through the port windows. The rain-soaked wind whipped back and forth as they held onto the braces in the hold. "Take skiffs two, three and five." Cholly Jake, the ship's engineer said gruffly. He pointed down the windy hold. "They all have almost full charges. They can take two people each over to that ship, and you can lock in each of the small explosives to cut their power. Make sure they're stuck in the right place, or we aren't going to have anything to show for all of this damned effort!"

Cholly was a rotund black man whose grey-shot hair stood

out plainly. He wasn't happy they were taking his boats, but if they didn't lock in that ship soon they would have to bail, and he agreed with Billy that they needed to be active now instead of just running a stern chase.

There was that large fleet that had raided New York a week back. The *Folly* avoided them, only to find that no one else was moving either. Everyone was waiting to see what happened.

Apparently, not too much had changed.

Cholly could hear the chatter going back and forth from the New York City-State Air Traffic Control, and everything seemed normal.

Now they had found one ship heading back to Europe, perhaps running with its tail between its legs.

He pointed to two of the crew. "You take number two." He pointed to the next two, a man and woman. "You take number three. You'll have to get over there within five minutes, but it should only take you sixty seconds. So, no becoming part of any mile-high club, Sled Three. Got that?"

They smiled. There wasn't enough room in those skiffs to change your mind, much less do anything physical. The pirates worked their way to the sleds.

3

ANTIGRAV SHIP *ARCHANGEL*

MICHAEL HAD all of his equipment on him. While he would have preferred to just do this without that burden, he didn't want to lose anything if for some reason the *ArchAngel* went down. He had already told Mark and Jacqueline to mentally scream his name if the ship started losing altitude, and he would come to their rescue as best he could.

Mark turned to Jacqueline and said, "Don't be calling Michael if you break a nail. I know how you women..." The crack of her backhand on his chest was impressive.

But Mark just smiled and took the blow. He rubbed his chest while Jacqueline pointed a finger at him. "You keep this up and you're going to be a twice-dead vampire. I don't care how hot you are." She left the room.

Michael looked at Mark, who winked at him as he tapped his head. "I've got her figured out."

The older vampire snorted and patted Mark on the shoulder.

"You might have the wolf figured out, but you have a serious logic flaw."

"What logic flaw?" Mark asked, frowning. Michael paused before leaving the room. "She's a woman. To believe there's logic in their actions and emotions is the first of many false assumptions."

Twenty minutes later Michael walked past the bridge and exited the protected area of the ship, continuing out to the open deck. The winds flowed around him from every direction.

The energy was whispering to him here in the storm. It wanted to be held, to be caressed, to be used and abused in an orgy of destruction.

Perhaps, Michael thought, *he was applying his own feelings to the weather.*

He had wanted only to sleep, and these imbeciles had taken that from him.

His coat whipped in the wind as he looked for the ship. A few seconds later he smiled, then took two steps and disappeared.

Above him, Mark watched his mentor leave and smirked.

Someone was going to get fucked up tonight.

Michael left the *ArchAngel* and took off in the direction of the pirate ship. The vibrations up here in the sky were a bit overwhelming, and he was having difficulty focusing on the ship's power source since he couldn't see it.

As he went one direction, he missed the two small power sources heading in from the other.

The ship drew nearer and the lights, powered by their own energy, flared into the clouds as they roiled around in the wind.

Michael solidified on the main deck and looked around. From time immemorial pirates had had a bad reputation, but many could and would be excellent at their jobs.

Almost like their lives depended on it.

Seeking out minds in the night, he found one man outside. He had hidden himself deep in the lee of the wind.

Michael grinned and glanced at the location of the man trying to hide from the weather. At his one job, to alert the ship should someone unknown attack them, he had failed.

His scream of death would tell those on this ship that something was not right.

Mark noticed the two lights approaching in the dark on his umpteenth scan, and grinned. He vacillated over whether he should inform Jacqueline they had incoming or not. On the one hand, he would have the chance to learn just how well he could throw those coming to attack them over the edge by himself.

Or, he could find out if Jacqueline would throw him off the ship in her annoyance at not being a part of the party.

Prudence won.

He double-checked the distance of the two attack ships and how carefully they were arriving, and decided going inside wasn't going to cut it. He reached over and grabbed a small metal bar, then tapped out a predetermined message. Three taps, pause. Two taps, pause.

One tap.

Mark checked that his weapons were secure, his knives in place and his pistol locked in. He had a coat now too, not quite the length of Michael's, but it helped hide most of his weaponry. He stood up and grabbed the ladder that allowed him to jump down to the deck of the ship, bracing himself as the wind whipped around him. With his hand on the rail he at least didn't worry about being flung out into the night by an unexpected gust of wind.

Then again, he wondered, *what gusts* were *expected*?

His landing was lost in the wind, and when Jacqueline opened the door it was only noticeable because of the light it threw out into the night, not from the sound.

Well, to a human.

Mark raised an eyebrow at his friend as she laughed at him.

"Are you shitting me?" she called out, looking around, "Someone is stupid enough to attack in this weather and Michael didn't kill them?"

Jacqueline scanned to starboard before she turned back to Mark and pointed a finger at him. "If you're fucking with me, I'll throw your skinny vampire ass off this ship! That would be no way to treat a lady."

Mark opened his mouth to reply but immediately had two feminine fingers pinching his lips closed. Jacqueline had moved next to him. "If you say one sentence that puts 'lady' and a disparaging remark together, these incoming pirates will have to take a back seat until after the ass-kicking I'll give you!"

Mark heard the wind shifting around new ships in the air before she did, so he looked to his left and raised his eyebrows. She never let go of his lips as she turned in the darkness. Seconds later, she caught the sound. Her fingers released his lips and she gave a tiny *squee* of delight in anticipation of fighting some pirates.

Mark rolled his eyes.

He reached inside his coat and verified again that all of the knives and the pistol were locked down. "I have the first to land. You take the second."

Jacqueline's head snapped around. "Who died and made you the boss?"

Mark smiled. "If you want to be included the next time bad guys come to play, you shouldn't act like a spoiled princess making demands."

Jacqueline frowned. If there was one thing she had learned about Mark since their first fateful meeting with Michael, it was that he could be annoyingly stubborn.

She had tried overwhelming him with nudity. That worked against her. Now, he probably could draw her naked from memory and she hadn't even seen a nice moon.

Fucking prudish vampires. The hot new body he had developed since getting Michael's blood and energy was driving her nuts.

So she tried to use her intelligence against him.

Fucking computer-hacking prudish vampires. The bastard was quite literate. Seems his type didn't go out much and he read all the time.

Finally, she tried to dominate him like an Alpha.

Fucking passive-aggressive computer-hacking prudish vampires. He wasn't dominated, he was just biding his time to assert his "you're not the boss of me" comments.

Which, she had to admit, *were damned hot.*

She needed to kill some pirates, then take a cold shower.

"What the hell was that?" Billy asked, hearing a shriek that didn't sound like it came from the wind buffeting the ship.

"Billy," Sally David called out, "I can't raise Tim outside."

"Stupid fucker is probably sleeping," Billy responded. "Why he wants nest duty in a storm is beyond me." He thought about it for a moment. "Tell Amanda and Arnold to go see what's up. Amanda 'cause she'll do it, and Arnold because she doesn't weigh more than fifteen pounds."

There were snickers around the bridge.

Michael switched back to Myst when he heard a door open. He had searched for an opening, but apparently these ships were more airtight than he would have given them credit for.

Two people came out, a man and a woman. The man was large, the woman in comparison, was quite small. Michael paused, they had something he wasn't expecting to find on a pirate ship.

They cared for each other.

In his Myst form, Michael pursed his lips, made a decision and stepped through the opening. He rematerialized and grabbed the door, yanking it from the man's grip and slamming it shut.

Locking the door from the inside, he turned around, ignoring the shouts of frustration from outside. He smiled at the first man to come around the corner, who was in shock that someone that he didn't recognize was on the ship.

A someone whose eyes were glowing red, and whose right hand was growing knives for nails.

Michael, pushing fear out to affect those throughout the ship, started down the hall to the first man. The guy's feet wouldn't obey as his mind screamed at him to run.

"You shall be my first tonight," Michael, his voice emotionless, told the man. "Honor needs to be fulfilled, and the fire is burning bright."

Outside on the deck, Arnold stopped beating on the door, but he tried again to yank it open when the screaming started. He kept one hand on the handle as a lifeline as the other arm reached out to scoop Amanda into his embrace. He could feel her hot tears of anger, and now fear, soaking his chest.

He might die tonight, but he would die trying to protect this fragile young woman.

ANTIGRAV SHIP *ARCHANGEL*

"SIR," scope operator Timms called over his shoulder to Captain Miles O'Banion. "Pirate ship is losing distance and changing direction."

Miles nodded before calling back, "Understood, Timms."

He reclined in the captain's chair and blew out a sigh. He now had to admit half of why he had been afraid of waking Michael himself.

When he chose to wake him up, Captain Miles O'Banion became guilty of murder. He might not be the one killing all of the men and women on the pirate ship behind them, but he knew what the end result would be.

"May God have mercy on their souls," he whispered to himself as he made the sign of the cross.

NEAR THE ANTIGRAV SHIP *ARCHANGEL*

"IF YOU DON'T like me suggesting sexual positions," Combs retorted to his partner on the trip over to the target ship, "maybe you shouldn't reply in kind!" He scowled as he piloted their two-person skiff towards their prize.

"Maybe," Juliana agreed from behind him, "but come on, there are sexual positions, then there are acrobatics, and then there's whatever the fuck you're actually suggesting. That shit isn't even remotely possible for a woman and there is absolutely no chance there could be any pleasure for her at all."

Combs thought about his last suggestion as he concentrated on their approach. The banter was helping him focus on the task at hand and ignore the buffeting winds as he punched the trigger to land on the ship's deck. A *clang* sounded as their metal skids connected and then locked tight with magnetics and gravity locks.

"All ashore who're going ashore," he called back as he made sure his weapons were locked in. He could hear Juliana doing the same. "Feel free to kill most everyone so our friends can catch up. Remember what Billy and Cholly said, we're scrapping this—"

Combs' get-ready speech was lost when someone knocked on the outside of the little craft. "What the fuck?" he shouted. He was wondering if he should hit the gravs and try to get back to the other ship when metal started squeaking, then squealing. Finally both he and Juliana froze, shocked as the brackets broke and the cockpit door was ripped off. A young man with blazing red eyes stood outlined against the darkness, the lights from their skiff illuminating him from the front, the lightning in the clouds silhouetting him from behind.

"Oh," he said to the two stricken pirates, "you *will* be going ashore." Combs tried to pull his pistol, and the young man reached down and slapped Combs' hand, breaking his wrist. He deftly unhooked the seat belts and grabbed Combs' shirt and belt.

Juliana, mouth open, heart beating wildly, watched as the vampire yanked Combs out of the chair. She heard his screams as he flew out and over the side of the ship.

Then those two red eyes turned to her and she saw her death written plainly.

She inhaled, trying to catch her breath. "But I'm a girl!"

The vampire didn't even smile; he merely unhooked her seatbelt and gripped her as he had Combs.

Before she was pulled from the ship and thrown over the side, she heard him say, "So was my sister."

Juliana closed her eyes, not wishing to know when the end would be. Just before she slammed into the sea, she wondered what the vampire's sister had done to him.

Back on the ship, Mark turned to see the second skiff hit the deck and Jacqueline approach it. He started walking towards it as well.

4

THE FLASH of the lightning was bright enough that it nearly blinded Terek as it vaporized Marc and Campbell's attack ship. "Land this fucking thing already or I'm going to throw up all over you!" he yelled. His partner Leon whooped and shouted as they flew from the *Folly* over to the prize.

"God damn, did you see the explosion? That could have been us!" Leon exclaimed.

"That isn't helping, Leon," Terek muttered as he refrained from slapping his pilot on the back of his head.

The *clang* of their landing did little for Terek's stomach. He patted himself down quickly, not caring too much about the loss of a couple items if he could just get the fuck out of this death trap.

He'd kick the shit out of Leon later.

The canopy on their little antigrav ship cracked, and he reached up to push. The damned thing absolutely couldn't open fast enough for him.

MICHAEL ANDERLE

The sudden *bang* from inside the canopy startled the shit out of him, as did the female bellowing right next to them.

"Motherfucker, that's my most comfortable shirt you just shot a hole in!"

Terek heard Leon scream as an arm reached into the cockpit and crushed his hand. His screams turned to gurgles when she hit him in the head three times, then chopped him in the neck once for each word she yelled.

"That. Hurt. You. Bastard!"

The fourth chop to Leon's throat caused his demise.

Terek was busy yanking out his pistol to shoot the woman. He looked up and saw her glowing yellow eyes, and knew immediately that he was fucked.

He had no silver bullets in his pistol. There weren't supposed to be any werewolves flying over the fucking sea, so who needed silver?

Apparently he did.

She had glanced over at him as she was beating the shit out of Leon, and didn't seem too worried. Terek found out why when another arm reached over and grabbed his wrist, easily breaking it and leaving the pistol hanging limply from fingers he couldn't control.

The screaming was now coming from his own mouth.

He grabbed his wrist and turned to look into the eyes of the male standing next to him. His spirit gave up. "Oh, fuck me!" Terek grunted when he saw the red glowing eyes.

"Not my type," the young vampire answered as he popped the seatbelt off, casually pulled him from the skiff, and tossed him, screaming, over the side of the ship.

"He's not?" Jacqueline asked as she unbuckled the first pirate and pulled him out of the little craft. She had to use both arms. "How the fuck did you make this seem so easy?" she grunted, then turned towards the edge of the deck and heaved the pirate's body back over her head, sending it off the side of the ship.

There was no yelling from that body.

Mark smiled and answered, "Practice."

Captain O'Banion swallowed as he and the others on the bridge watched the casual way the two took out the four pirates. No one said a word, but they all could feel fear mixed with gratitude.

Without them they might have had deaths on the ship, as they fought pirates they wouldn't have known were sneaking aboard.

Who tries to land those damned antigrav skiffs in a storm? There was no one stupid enough to try that.

Well, except these pirates who had just met the welcoming party, and then been casually thrown off the ship to their deaths. Including the one that Jacqueline had beaten the shit out of for shooting her.

"I think the young woman is going to need food," Miles said into the quiet of the bridge. "Timms, take care of that. Someone also needs to make sure that Mark is okay. I didn't see if he got hurt, but we need to make sure." The Captain turned to Sasha, who had seemed interested in the vampire before. "Can you check on how Mark is doing?"

This time, the infatuation Sasha usually displayed when talking about Mark was absent.

It had been replaced with fear.

THE PIRATE SHIP *FOLLY*

MICHAEL HAD SPENT the better part of fifteen minutes locating the heartbeats, heavy breathing, and finally the people who were producing both.

Twice he had heard gunshots that didn't come near him. He

later found two who had taken their own lives. He made the sign of the cross over their bodies.

They had come to grips with their own sins and paid the final price.

Now he had only the engine room to deal with. He walked down the hallway and started walking slowly down the ladder to the lower level.

Thump, thump, thump, thump, thump.

Behind him, the ship was deathly quiet.

Cholly Jake hadn't been able to raise the bridge in over five minutes. That told him all he needed to know.

The Antichrist had found them, just like his mother had predicted thirty years before on her deathbed.

"You be careful you not be doing what you ain't supposed to be!" she had said, "or the dark Christ will take you out one day!"

He was busy wrapping the wire around his dead-man switch as his mind replayed that last conversation, the touch of his mother's hand caressing his cheek as a tear tracked down the cheek of the younger version of him.

He reached up and wiped a similar one off.

"I might be joining you soon, Mom," he whispered. "But I won't go down without taking the devil with me."

He pulled hard, seating the wire, then turned around as the steps came closer to his engine room.

It was a shame he wouldn't be able to see the explosion from the outside. He had always wanted to know what happened when you fused all of the power in an antigrav core.

Amanda shivered against Arnold and spoke into his chest. "The screaming has stopped."

When the sound died, so had the fear. Arnold felt like the danger was moving away from them now.

Not that he could do one damned thing about it.

He had been trying to figure out how they could get inside, and the only solution he could see was using some of the equipment to break the windows to get back into the ship. Well, Amanda could get back in.

He was too big for that.

Plus, he could probably hold her high enough over the sharp edges to protect her. He would get cut, but with some care, nothing too bad. Then she could let him inside.

He was trying to figure out what might work when the ship dropped probably ten feet, causing them to slam down on the deck.

"Oh, fuck," Arnold whispered.

There was no way he would be able to save her from a fall that high.

"I know you're here!" Cholly yelled, his eyes darting around the engine room. "I'm ready to answer for my sins. Are you?"

The maddening voice came back calm, cool and unhurried. "If I *could* die, I would have a long time ago, Cholly Jake."

"How the hell do you know my name?" Cholly looked around to make sure the bastard hadn't slipped behind him somehow. His left hand gripped the dead-man switch feverishly. "You know neither of us are getting out of this, right?"

"No, Cholly Jake," the voice replied, "I'm not sure of that."

Cholly licked his lips. "My momma warned me about you, but I didn't believe her. We all thought she was slightly damaged in the brain. The stories she would tell after her dreaming!"

"Stories? People have told dream stories for centuries, Cholly. I should know, I've heard them for over a thousand years."

Cholly whispered a curse as he decided to let go. A viselike grip wrapped around his hand on the dead-man switch, keeping his hold tight.

"Now," the voice whispered to Cholly, who had closed his eyes expecting the ship to blow apart. "The problem with a device like this is the person you are playing with might be able to read your thoughts."

Cholly opened one fearful eye and took in the visage of the man in front of him. He was holding a sword in his right hand, his left hand wrapped around Cholly's own.

He grinned at Cholly.

"If that person can read your thoughts, he will know if you intend to truly kill yourself, and when. Then he gets to stop you." Michael looked down at the dead-man switch. "You won't be needing this anymore."

Michael slashed down, severing Cholly's hand at the wrist. He moved to Cholly's left so he was out of the way of the spurting blood as the man screamed, grabbing his bleeding stump and dropping to his knees.

"So, dead-man switches only work—"

The ship dropped suddenly, and Cholly gasped as he lost his balance. Michael looked around and back at the switch. He chewed his lip and finished his statement, "if you release the button, or do a piss-poor job making them in the first place, dammit!"

The ship dropped a second time and Cholly looked back to grin at the man. Looked like Cholly was going to win, with or without his hand.

Except the devil wasn't there anymore.

Arnold let go of the door handle to hold Amanda in his arms.

"Why now, you big ox?" her muffled voice cried. "Now that we're going to die, you have the courage to hold me?"

"I've told you before," he answered, playing with her hair for a moment until the ship lurched again. They sprawled back ten feet. Arnold yelled for Amanda and grabbed her leg. There was a *clang* from the door as it slammed open.

Good thing they weren't there, or they would absolutely be dead at the moment.

Then, he felt Amanda, himself and—another—as they floated away from the ship. Arnold's vision was focused on the ship as they sped away. As the ship fell, it turned black and shrank for a split second, then shattered and exploded. An invisible wave caused a massive disturbance in the clouds around the ship before it was lost to his sight.

"Arnold?" Amanda's voice called out, gentle in the night.

"I'm here, Amanda," he replied, trying to get a lock on where her voice was coming from.

That's when a third voice entered their conversation, and Arnold's blood, assuming he still had any, froze.

—

"The two of you," the male voice told them, "are all that is left of the *Folly*."

Amanda tried to keep ahold of her courage and asked, "Are you Death?"

The chuckle that came back to them didn't reassure Amanda at all, but his words did. "No, although some have called me different versions of Death over the centuries. My name is Michael."

Amanda interrupted, "You're the ArchAngel!"

There was a pause in the communication. "No, not the Arch-Angel Michael you're thinking of. I am not Christianity's High Angel for God."

"But, you saved us when you could have easily killed us for being on the ship," Amanda argued. Arnold fell in love again with her voice, the purity of her heart evident in her simple questions. Not that *she* was simple, but she never failed to ask the questions. "Why?"

Michael kept one part of his mind focused on the power sources to facilitate the return to the *ArchAngel* as he pondered her question. *Why had he saved them?* The old Michael would have killed everyone and not thought twice about it. They were on a pirate ship, obviously then trusted by the pirates.

His voice softened. "Because love is more powerful than deceit and selfishness. One cannot love as you two do, not only each other but also family and friends, and be truly evil." They continued to speed towards the ship barely discernible in the clouds. "And because I myself have been changed by love, and I'll stay on the path as best I can."

They allowed their host's answer to wash over them as they pondered what the hell they were doing when it seemed the Heavens opened and God's own lightning surrounded them.

The ship they were approaching was hit multiple times, and as their speed increased, Arnold noticed an explosion in the aft section.

Right where the antigrav technology should be located.

5

OVER THE PACIFIC

"FIND ME THAT SHIP," Akio snapped. While their technology was substantial, even with a hundred and fifty-plus years of improvements since Bethany Anne had left, they had trouble locating a ship in a storm over the ocean. Separating the power sources from the large natural disturbances was not something Eve had developed any algorithms for yet.

"I am trying, Akio-*san*," Eve answered. This time, Akio detected a bit of fluctuation in her answer.

He was stressing the AI too much. Akio pondered his obligations to everyone in a blistering second. His honor to his Queen. His responsibility to Eve, and his friendship, he realized, with both of them.

The grim line of his lips said he was surprised at himself, if you knew this man well enough to tell.

Akio had an AI as a friend. Over fifteen decades, and only now was he willing to accept even he could learn a new trick or two.

"Do not stress, Eve," he said. "We will be successful, the Queen is assured."

Eve, her voice back on track, responded, "We lost the ability to speak to the Queen a long time ago, Akio. How can you be certain?"

"Little one, it is time I teach you," he said, his reflexes pulling the ship he was piloting hard to the side as he dodged clouds that seemed to be roiling more than usual, "about a human concept called faith."

ANTIGRAV SHIP ARCHANGEL

"THE FACT that you took out two other people should have alerted you to the fact the second asshole pirate was mine!" yelled Jacqueline.

Mark and Jacqueline were still arguing out on the deck. Each had a hand on the pirates' second craft. Captain O'Banion had tried to call them in after their successful eviction of the pirates. When he opened the door to talk to them, they both turned to look at him.

One pair of red eyes, one pair of yellow.

Family arguments weren't his problem. He shouted, "Thank you!" and shut the door. He told those who had been ready, if not exactly willing, to help them that they could go back to their tasks. Those two were arguing with each other and it was best to let them get the arguing out of their system.

Five minutes later, all hell broke loose.

"What the fuck?" Jacqueline screeched as the ship lurched to the side. Both she and Mark slammed their other hands onto the slip of a ship and grabbed hold.

Jacqueline failed to grab anything useful. A second and third bolt of lightning cracked, the sound blasting through their heightened senses, and the electricity ran through all of the metal on the deck. The ship's capacity for capturing errant lightning bolts had been temporarily overwhelmed.

Mark grabbed Jacqueline's free hand, locking on as if he would be her safety belt. He easily moved her whole body to place her second hand on a bar.

"Goddammit!" he yelled at her. "Don't you fucking think about falling off or I'll jump after you and cuss you out the whole way down!"

Jacqueline's expression was one of maniacal glee as the adrenaline hit her. They enjoyed the wild ride as the humans inside fought to keep their ship afloat in the sky.

"Not if you fall first, Vamp Boy!"

Then one last lightning bolt hit the ship and both of them screamed in incredible pain.

Michael saw his two charges out in the storm, arguing by a boat he knew hadn't been there when he had left the ship. He had obviously failed to detect the intruders on the way to the pirates' ship. He wanted to roll his eyes in frustration.

Didn't they realize they were in a *Gott Verdammt* storm?

They needed to get over their damned issues and become friends or partners or something. This dancing around was for the young.

Which unfortunately, they were.

God, he missed Bethany Anne.

The ship was in trouble and he had to make a fast decision. Considering their height, he could catch it before they hit the seas below.

He took the two humans onto the ship and rematerialized in the middle of the bridge.

"What do you mean we lost the left bank of batteries?" the captain yelled as he helped his first mate get back to his feet. The engineer's voice replied over the speaker, "I mean we blew out our capacitors and they sunk the power safely to the grounds. Unless you got a handy recharging unit, Captain, we just lost half our power!"

Miles ground his teeth. Losing half their power meant they were effectively screwed. He would need to decide whether continuing on would be better, or just to let the ship go down. The storm had been heading west, so trying to retreat would just putting them back in its path. Maybe the girl had been right, and waking the vampire is what he should have done. Now he had damned everybody.

That's when three people materialized on his bridge.

The shared pain from his charges pissed Michael off, so his sudden appearance—eyes glowing as bright as those on the bridge had ever seen—wasn't the gentle arrival he had hoped to accomplish.

"These two," Michael said, "are good people. Find out what they can do and use them. I'm done with this fucking storm." With that declaration, he pivoted and exited the bridge.

The captain looked at the people Michael had dropped, their confusion matching his own.

"Okay," the captain barked, "what did you do on your ship?"

Michael left the bridge through the hatch to the deck. He turned the lock and slammed it shut.

His two charges, he noticed, looked weak, but seemed to be dealing with their sudden electrocution.

He darted over to them and pressed his hands together, rubbing them and willing the power to generate. There was no waiting or coercing. This time it *would* obey him.

Or he would go into the Etheric and rip that dimension a new asshole.

He pressed a hand against both Mark and Jacqueline, pushing

energy to them to allow their nanocytes to heal them. Mark recovered first, his eyes darting to Jacqueline. He noticed Michael's hand on her and moved his gaze up the arm to Michael himself.

Mark swallowed. He was apparently in no mood to talk.

Jacqueline gasped a breath, then moaned. "Oh God that fucking huurrrrtttt." Her eyes popped open. She looked over to see who was touching her, then back at Mark.

She slapped his arm. "What the hell, Mark? What did you do to get us electrocuted?"

"You two," Michael growled, his voice richer and deeper than normal. They peered at him, but he was looking up at the clouds, his face a mask of extreme displeasure. "Just kiss and get it over with."

He stood up, noticing neither Jacqueline's surprise nor Mark's narrowed-eyed look of determination.

The captain sent the new people down to the engine room. Apparently they had worked there on the other ship, being useless anywhere else. They wouldn't fight, but ability to work with technology trumped bloodthirsty every time.

Miles watched Michael help his two charges, then stand up and stride to the middle of the deck. Michael looked around as if he were seeing something no one else could.

All at once his eyes flashed red, bright enough to cast shadows as he threw his arms into the air. Blue energy left his hands to attack the weather, but lightning fought back and struck him. Mother Nature was not pleased with him, and didn't take to his machinations to manipulate her will lying down.

Michael ignored the disintegration of his body as the Etheric healed him at the atomic level. He had spent over a hundred years inside the Etheric being put back together molecule by molecule.

He and the Etheric were old associates. Perhaps not friends, but certainly intimate nonetheless.

Michael kept his hands raised, pulling in the power of the storm and shunting it into the Etheric. At the same time, he pushed power back out into the air to change the temperature.

He was in the center, screaming at the storm. Although close, neither Jacqueline nor Mark could hear as they clutched each other. The power being unleashed mere steps from them was more than their minds could take in.

"You think you're worse than an atomic bomb?" Michael screamed, "YOU NEED TO BRING MORE THAN THIS!"

So Mother Nature hit him with three lightning bolts at once as he pulled in power.

"THAT TICKLES, BITCH!" he shouted back. If he had thought about it, he would have had to admit he was lying.

The pain was enormous.

His eyes narrowed, he reinforced his will, his voice a whisper, "I promised her I would be back. I *am* the Dark Messiah, I *am* the ArchAngel, but more than that, my name is Michael Nacht and I stayed together for her. You are in no way more powerful than *my fucking love*." Michael grinned maniacally as he remembered his friends from the past and what they might say in such a situation as this.

"SUCK IT!" he yelled, and started laughing as he pushed more Etheric energy into the atmosphere. The lightning became less frequent, and the winds started decreasing.

Bethany Anne certainly wouldn't get the same Michael back, but all things considered?

That was a good thing.

THE DUKE'S **Residence in Germany**

LIGHTNING FLASHED TWICE before a low boom of thunder could be felt by the human guiding the large antigrav vehicle through the narrow brick walls of the estate to the landing pad inside.

His face was soaked from the rain, but it would have been wet with sweat even had the weather been dry.

The last person in this position had failed to keep their focus and the vehicle had scraped against the wall on the way in.

The Duke had ripped the flagman's head off and licked the blood from his neck in front of a good portion of those in the castle that night.

There were many outside of this building that did not understand just what the Duke was. But those within these walls were very aware, and were either here because they had sworn loyalty, or…

Because they were slaves.

Bryon Donnington had started out a believer, but it had only taken two weeks to understand the lie he had been fed. He wasn't the follower of a great man, but of a monster. To keep his own head on his shoulders now, he needed to stop thinking about useless shit in the middle of a storm and make sure this damned vehicle made it down without scratching the paint.

Moments later, he flagged the driver to kill the engines. He saluted the car with a hand over his heart as he had been taught half a year back, then turned and walked towards his quarters in the Duke's castle.

William 'Duke' Renaud strode through the doors, which closed behind him. With hours to go until sunrise, he scowled at the weather. No sun to stop him from enjoying the outdoors, but he wasn't willing to get his clothes soaked by staying outside.

He glanced at the map on the large table in his planning room as he walked in. A fraction of a moment later he stopped, then pivoted to his left and took three steps to look over the large map of Europe. He frowned and reached up to tap his lips as he concentrated on what had changed in the past four nights.

He spoke at slightly above a normal level. "Gerard?"

Seconds later a man approached the door and bowed. "Yes sir?"

The Duke pointed at the map. "Why are we missing two pack tokens in Paris?"

The man answered, "Sir, I was informed by Terrance that the leaders of packs Leleuand and Duval have not been back to the staging area outside of Paris in the last three nights."

His master continued tapping his lips. "So, you believe they have decided to break the agreement?"

"I cannot say at the moment if they will remain absent, my lord. However, they have officially missed two meetings in three days."

The Duke nodded his understanding. "We have the firstborn child of the Alphas of both the Leleuand and Duval packs, correct?"

"That is correct, sir."

"Good." The Duke turned back to his original direction and started walking towards a side exit. "Do pull those two children out and videotape them being served to the Nosferatu, Gerard."

Gerard nodded to the rapidly retreating shadow as he closed the doors to the planning room. "Very good, sir."

Less than five minutes later, the Duke could hear the screams of fear as the two teenagers were pulled from their rooms. He smiled.

One mustn't hesitate to mete out punishment; respect was so easily lost.

His grandfather, Michael, had taught him that just before he had been entombed by the same man.

6

JAPAN

YUKO FLUTTERED AROUND THE BASE. Eve followed her and asked more questions than the usually patient Yuko cared to answer.

The little android stopped in exasperation as Yuko used the rag in her hand to wipe the top of a frame that had been on the hallway's wall for the last two decades.

Eve pointed back down the hall. "This is as close to clean as we can get unless you wish to re-clean everything which hasn't been touched in the last two days."

Yuko ran the white cloth across the top of the picture and glanced at it.

Clean.

"So," Eve continued, her hands on her waist. "Why are you cleaning again?"

Yuko turned to consider her friend and sighed. "If I have nothing to do, my mind runs scenarios about what might happen should Michael arrive and it isn't perfect."

"You think he will care about dust on top of a picture frame?" Eve asked.

"No… Yes…" Yuko blew out a breath of air. "Eve, how long have we been waiting for him?"

"Exactly—" Eve started.

"Stop!" Yuko put up a hand. "That was meant to be rhetorical, not a request for exact information. I have no need to be reminded of how old I am."

"Which is why we celebrate your twenty-sixth birthday each year."

"Yes, that was a good year," Yuko admitted.

"What was his name?"

Yuko eyed the AI. "You know what his name was, but you are fishing for Akio's name for him."

"Available," the AI answered.

"Sometimes, for a wonderful friend you can be such a bitch." Yuko huffed and started towards the living quarters.

"Perhaps," Eve said. *But you aren't thinking about Michael arriving right now, are you?*

Antigrav Ship *ArchAngel*

Jacqueline grabbed Mark's hand and held on tight as she shielded her eyes from the constant barrage of searing light.

"Stop it, Michael" she yelled for what had to be the hundredth time. She cried out in frustration and gave up, rolling into the crook of Mark's arm. She sobbed into his chest. "He's going to die!"

Mark couldn't see anything just then, his irises were regenerating after he made the mistake of trying to watch what was happening without eye protection. With one hand clamped on the pirates' skiff and the other arm holding Jacqueline, he had nothing left to cover the brightness.

Then his curiosity got the better of him, and he tried to blink quickly to catch just a small glimpse of what the Pinnacle of Vampires was doing. It burned his eyes out in a flash... literally.

He sure hoped nothing happened to the ship in the next few moments while his eyes healed.

Mark wasn't sure if Michael would truly be killed, but he sincerely doubted it. Michael had yet to seem impulsive. Mad, angry, irritated, short of temper, impatient, infuriating, incensed, enraged and occasionally annoyed.

But never impulsive.

"He's just having a good time," Mark yelled back to Jacqueline, hoping he got close to where her ear was. Moments later he could see her outline, and he smiled.

An outline was better than sheer white.

"Well, for having a good time, he's scaring the hell out of me!" she snapped back.

"C'mon Jacqueline, it isn't every day you get to be in the center of a storm," Mark replied, his voice calming as he realized that the claps of thunder and other sounds resulting from Michael's struggle had dropped off. He looked around, his mouth opening when he saw huge gaps in the clouds and swaths of blue showing everywhere.

Mark saw Michael with his arms crossed like he was daring someone to do something. Mark smiled as he turned to see who Michael was looking at, and his smile faded.

He nudged Jacqueline. "You need to turn around, J," Mark urged. "We got more company."

"What?" Jacqueline turned to see what Mark was talking about, the ringing in her ears annoying the shit out of her as they healed.

That's when her mouth dropped open as well. "Mark, why is there a black spaceship facing off with Michael?"

"Fuck if I know," Mark whispered. "But as badass as that ship looks, I'm still going with Team Michael."

Jacqueline nodded, not noticing her subconscious effort to keep her body pressed against Mark's.

Akio, long time, Michael sent.

Hai, Akio replied.

Is there something you need at the moment, or are you just planning on hanging out there off the side of the ship? More to the point, where is Bethany Anne?

She took the fight to the Kurtherians.

Michael pursed his lips. *How long?*

Over one hundred and fifty years ago, My Lord.

Michael raised an eyebrow. *My Lord?*

Akio's smirked for a moment. *It seemed appropriate, considering all of the power I just registered inbound to this ship. It doesn't look damaged, though.*

Michael saw that the vampire and the werewolf were still clutching each other. "This is Akio, one of the Queen's Bitches." Michael walked towards the skiff they weren't holding onto. He yanked up the canopy, looked at the controls, and reached in to flip one of the switches.

Nothing.

He grimaced and looked a second time. He moved two switches to the left and pulled up on the red one as well, and felt the small magnetic connectors disconnect from the decking.

Michael called, "Mark, Jacqueline, come here!"

They pulled away from each other and jogged over to where Michael was squatting beside the small ship. He pointed Mark to the back and Jacqueline to the front.

"On three," Michael told them. Both reached to grab a portion of the ship, then Michael spoke.

"Three!"

The three nanocyte-modified humans tossed the little ship

into the air, easily missing the larger airship as they heaved it off the deck.

Mark watched it tumble out of sight. "Sure hope we don't need that."

Akio, come, Michael sent as he turned to the other two. "Akio needs to land, so let's move away from this part of the deck."

"Akio?" Mark asked.

"The Dark One?" Jacqueline demanded.

Michael raised an eyebrow at Jacqueline as she watched the silent ship turn in the air as it worked to settle on the deck.

Jacqueline and Mark carefully didn't ask Michael how much it hurt for half of his face to be regenerating. She could see the white of bone on his skull and along the left side of his jaw as he talked.

Whatever Michael had just done, she imagined a large part of his body was being rebuilt, she for one was glad he hadn't been killed.

But God, it just had to have hurt.

"Captain," his first mate whispered as those on the bridge stood transfixed, watching the umpteenth strange occurrence in the last week float about the height of a man above the deck.

Captain Miles O'Banion turned to look at the screen, then glanced through the port window to see how the clouds were dispersing.

"Just consider it par for the course," he answered.

"What?" The first mate turned to see the captain gazing out the window. "No sir, look at the batteries, sir."

Miles looked over to his right and raised his eyebrows in surprise. The banks of batteries were both in the green.

Miles reached over and hit the call switch. "Engineering?"

"Aye sir," the male voice answered. "I thought you might be calling."

"I am," Miles replied. "The readout up here says we have enough power to make it to Europe."

"We do, Captain."

"Thank you." Miles let go of the switch, then bent to press it again and asked, "How are those two we sent you working out?"

It took a moment before his answer came back. "I'm not sure how you got 'em, but I aim to keep 'em so keep your captain hands off of 'em, okay?"

Miles smiled. "I'll take that under advisement."

He released the call button and started towards the hatch. "I'll be back. I've got to see this up close."

Michael waited patiently as the sleek black Pod kept pace with the antigrav ship and landed on the deck. He smirked to himself.

He could feel the muscles in his jaw knit back together as he waited for Akio to exit the Pod.

Jacqueline was having a hard time not staring at Michael's body in fascination, and Mark was busy examining the black ship.

Mark had a choice between watching a human rebuilding himself from the atoms of the Universe, a hot girl standing right next to him, or a black ship with weapons. He chose the ship.

He was a geek for sure.

Michael's face was completely healed by the time Akio jumped out of his ship, walked over and then bowed to him. Michael returned the gesture. He noticed Mark bowing too, and elbowing Jacqueline to follow suit.

"Akio," Michael said.

"My liege," Akio replied, gaining a smile from Michael.

"Still trying to figure out how to address me?" Michael asked the younger man as he turned to point to the two youngsters. "The one focused on the ship is Mark, and the one focused on you is Jacqueline." Akio exchanged pleasantries with them as Michael added, "The one coming out of the hatch in a second is this ship's captain, Miles O'Banion."

Mark, Jacqueline and Akio turned as the door opened. Miles found three sets of eyes on him. Everyone's except Michael.

The captain took a moment to allow the door to close behind him, then continued towards them. "Sorry?"

Michael turned. "No need, Captain O'Banion. This gentleman is an old friend of mine, who has come here under orders."

Jacqueline interjected, "Orders?"

"Yes," Michael responded. "He was ordered to find me."

"How does anyone know you're here?" Mark asked, curious.

Akio turned to the young man. "My Queen was very explicit that I was to wait until the Patriarch chose to show up."

"Like, how long?" Jacqueline asked.

Akio looked at her and raised an eyebrow.

Jacqueline tried to figure out why he was quiet. "Sir?"

"It has been over one hundred and fifty years," he answered, his lips quirking in a small grin.

"Fuuuuuck!" Jacqueline turned to Michael. "What did you do to her that she sent someone to find you a hundred and fifty years later?"

This time, Michael could sense the amusement Akio was sending his way, even if his face showed no emotions. Michael considered a new challenge in his life. He was going to get the stiff man to open up. He couldn't stay walking around as if he had a sword stuck up his ass for the next hundred years. Especially if he was going to be around all the time. "I believe," Michael answered Jacqueline, "that she loves me."

"You?" Jacqueline shot back in surprise. Both Mark and the captain put their hands over their mouths.

"And you find this hard to believe, why?" he asked as he adjusted his left pants leg so it wouldn't get caught in the skin as the last of his muscles regenerated.

His clothes were going to have to be cleaned for sure.

"Well, um." She looked back at Mark, who was still checking

out the ship, before she looked back at Michael. "I suppose she's a badass too. Takes one to know one?"

"You could say she's a real bitch," Michael agreed, "but you had better say it with deference."

"If I may interrupt?" The captain's voice came from behind them and they all looked back. "It seems we have plenty of power to make it to Europe now." He gazed at the sky. "You also seem to have taken care of the weather."

"I was still a bit upset," Michael said, admitting nothing more.

"Right." Miles said. "Where would you like to go next?"

Michael turned back to Akio. "Let's talk."

7

"WHERE THE HELL—" THE CAPTAIN HAD STARTED TO ASK AS HE looked around in surprise. Mark moved to put his hand against Miles' mouth.

"Don't say anything," Mark cautioned. "Just because he disappeared with Akio doesn't mean he might not be right next to us."

"Or a hundred yards off the ship," Jacqueline added, as Mark turned to look at her. "*Damn* he can be annoying."

"You wanted to sneak a listen to his plans?" Mark's eyebrows raised in mock astonishment.

"Yup." Jacqueline was unrepentant.

"What plans?" the captain asked.

"Whether he's leaving in that plane," she answered, pointing to the sleek black vessel.

Mark got down on his knees and looked under the Pod. "It isn't even touching the deck."

The captain bent at the waist to confirm Mark's statement. "Have you ever heard of such technology?"

"Yes," Jacqueline said. "My father told me about it when I was a little girl." She walked over to the black Pod and ran a hand along its sides. "This is some of the original technology of Bethany Anne's team. The Queen Bitch's stuff."

"Your father?" Miles asked, coming up behind her but not willing to touch the craft himself.

"Yes. He was alive before the world died, Captain." she whispered. "Bethany Anne is Michael's Queen, as well as his love. She asked him to protect a military base in the middle of the old United States as she fought someone in Eastern Europe, I think. My ancient history for Michael is a bit dodgy."

Jacqueline looked inside the canopy, but didn't go into the ship. She thought she knew how much she could get away with when pushing Michael, but this new vampire was different. He seemed too controlled for her liking, and she wasn't going to test him.

Yet.

"Why didn't she take him with her to wherever she is, then?"

Jacqueline turned around. "Because he died."

"What?" he asked, looking around for Michael on the deck of the ship. "How many times can he die, and how did he come back?"

"Apparently," she answered, "he had promised on his honor that he would come back to her, and she believed him. He was killed by a small nuclear explosion. My father was very insistent that he tell me the stories of vampires and how to keep my mouth shut around them."

Mark snorted. "He didn't do a very good job."

Jacqueline's melancholy caught Mark by surprise. "He tried, but I wasn't a willing learner."

Jacqueline turned to lean her back against Akio's craft. "Did you see what he did out here, Captain?"

He nodded.

"Did you see his face when you came out, and was it whole?"

"I saw his face," the captain explained, turning to his left to nod up at the bridge's windows. "From up there. There wasn't half of it left, I thought."

Mark added, "Well, he healed some then by the time I saw it."

"Yes, but the ability to regenerate that he demonstrated right now isn't like a vampire," Jacqueline told him.

"Well—" Mark interrupted.

"Okay," Jacqueline agreed, "not a normal vampire. Even Mark can accomplish some of what Michael is doing, which is healing through the Etheric, and that ability is unique to vampires." She was quiet a moment before adding, "I wondered how come it never seemed like he needed to eat."

My Liege, Akio's voice spoke into the Myst as Michael took them up a hundred feet above the *ArchAngel*.

I just wanted to get away from them for a moment. They need to calm down from the experience together, and I believe the captain is a better anchor for them right now.

Hai.

What were Bethany Anne's orders to you, Akio?

We were to wait, and be prepared to help you upon your return.

Michael thought a moment. *Are you in contact with her?*

No. We thought we would be able to communicate once they went through the Yollin Gate, but it was destroyed and we have had only very, very short communications between Eve and Adam. We are reduced to simple five-digit sends approximately every six months.

Have you notified her of my arrival?

No. Not until we were sure we had you safe.

Safe is subjective, Akio.

My King, Akio had started to speak when he felt Michael's amusement at Akio's search for the right honorific. *We have access to you, and I will work with you now to keep you safe.*

I have a meeting I must attend in Europe.

May I ask with whom?

A vampire calling himself the Duke. Michael could feel Akio's annoyance. *You know of him?*

Yes, I have recently found out about his activity. It is a significant mark against my honor that it has taken me this long to realize that such a powerful vampire is working in Europe and has acquired a large number of resources.

How many is large?

Eve and Yuko have yet to confirm, but certainly in the thousands of nanite-enhanced, Sir.

Apparently, Michael thought, *calling him King didn't make Akio's cut, either.*

Akio, I'm Michael, no more, no less. I expect your obedience, I will not knowingly countermand your orders from Bethany Anne, but I will not allow this Duke to continue accumulating power. I met his daughter in New York, and his son.

The one named Valerie, yes?

That is correct. You have met her?

Hai. *I spoke with her when seeking you, and Yuko and I helped in New York.*

Is there something that should be done for her?

Not at this time. She must stand on her own, or she will expect the mother bird to help her fly every time.

Michael didn't answer for a moment, then agreed. *Standing on her own worked for Bethany Anne. Give me a quick summary of what has happened since I unexpectedly left, please.*

Akio explained the rise of TQB, space, the Yollins and the gate, the world going against Bethany Anne and how they took the fight through the gate.

Akio waited a few moments before asking, *I presume we will be taking down the Duke?*

Of course. I will not allow his dishonor to continue, Akio.

It will be thousands against the two of us, sir.

Michael smirked in the Myst.

It's four of us, Akio. And finally I'll be able to allow Jacqueline her fill of fighting and I'll still have plenty of fools to play with myself.

Akio watched as they started back down to the ship.

Michael supposed this ship might be considered *ArchAngel 0*, since the original, *ArchAngel I*, had gone to the stars and was far superior to this craft. He guessed he was being a little romantic in wanting a ship named after one his love had flown out into the beyond.

Or he really was self-absorbed, to name a ship after himself. While the information was belated, he preferred to think he was romantic over the truth.

Inside a Secret Location In France

William Renaud had spent the better part of his slow atrophy toward death in a tomb, planning what he would do should he ever get the chance to live again.

Two grave robbers had given him that chance after the fall of mankind and the rise of the paranormal. He remembered the moment again, as his agitated mind cast about.

The tomb Michael had chosen was in a mountainside, with granite walls and floor. William had tried to dig his way to freedom, and so had been obliged to regrow his fingers over and over again. He had finally despaired. Instead of seeking to understand his selfish ambitions, he had instead spent his time exploring the power which made him more than human.

More than those who were rightly beneath him.

He ignored the desire to continue to fight his sentence, and chose to believe that the future was where he should focus. So, he reviewed the tomb and set traps in good locations. Traps to capture the mind of any who might find this place, to bring them to him in. William suspected he would be weak when he awoke—if he awoke—and would need the distance they had to travel from the cave entrance to subjugate his food.

In the end, it hadn't been needed.

The two grave robbers had been frozen in place, barely able to scream in fear when they woke William with their delicious scents of both food and freedom. He had been able to enjoy the first, Enzo, as pitiful screams filled his ears with their delightful sounds while his legs and arms thrashed around. His partner Elliot finally had found the ability to move and tried to run.

Too little, too late.

William had walked easily over to the youth as he crawled, crying, across the floor towards the entrance that opened to the one thing he needed most.

Freedom.

He could hear nothing outside as the sobbing boy tried to escape.

William grabbed him by the foot when the entrance was just a body length away and dragged him screaming back into the cave so he could rest forever next to his friend.

Together in death as they had been together in life.

It took two days for William's body to heal using the fresh infusion of blood. While Enzo's clothes might have fit him, they were too bloody to wear, unfortunately.

"I do apologize," William had told the body, face fused in a rictus of fear, "for my bad table manners. I was much more patient with your friend Elliot." William had pointed to his partner. "His clothes are a bit small, but I believe I might have other options soon," he said to the two unhearing bodies as he stripped Elliot of his clothes.

"So very soon."

It took William a month of capturing and killing humans to realize that the world he had been reborn in was both more and less advanced than the one Michael had shut him away from.

So he set about learning more, to enhance himself and gain the ability to create his own progeny. His daughter Valerie had been an unexpected surprise. His own father, who had been banned as Forsaken over a century before his demise, had explained how useless trying to turn a female would be. William had gotten it right the first time and never tried again. Why challenge his perfect record?

His other early child was a man, and when the two children fought, he could sense the strength of Valerie against Donovan.

She had the spirit to win, but Donovan had the necessary understanding that life wasn't fair and the willingness to do what it took to conquer.

William had spent decades training Valerie before he set her on her path. She would either make it in this new future or die.

She broke, and then she died.

He was sure Donovan had been involved in her death, but William had been too focused on his own efforts to attain power over the humans, with their technology and society, to keep fully abreast of what was going on.

Then it became time to send Donovan to New York City-State and that was what bothered him now. He had received no reports of Donovan's success.

The bed squeaked as William got up and padded to his shower to clean off. His mind was troubled, and from the centuries in the tomb, he knew what that meant.

The future was agitated.

He needed to leave this location and seek safety. Whatever had happened in New York had failed and he needed to go to ground elsewhere and determine what was bothering him.

He needed to feel the safety of earth and stone around him once more.

"Gerard!" he yelled. Moments later his trusted servant rapped on the door.

"Sir?"

William called out as he toweled dry, "Prepare the main car and the diversion. We are leaving as soon as it is dark."

8

ANTIGRAV SHIP *ARCHANGEL*, OVER THE ATLANTIC

INSIDE THE MEETING ROOM, the ancient map was laid out on the table. Akio was pointing out different locations.

"Here and here in Germany, here in England and at least here and here," Akio tapped two locations, "in France."

Michael nodded slowly. "So, a minimum of five locations where the Duke could be, and if he is who I think he might be, he'll have more."

He looked towards Akio. "What assets do you have in space?"

"Space?" Mark's voice interrupted quickly, followed by the sound of Jacqueline's slap.

"Shhh!" she hissed. The two men ignored their whispered conversation.

"We have four satellites available. The rest have decomposed or we have lost them over the decades. They will do searches to see if we can ascertain location, but it could take us a while to confirm a specific location since he has antigrav vehicles."

"How… annoying," Michael replied.

Akio simply shrugged.

The captain sat in a corner listening to the two vampires speak about technologies, times, cities and history that he had never expected to hear about from two who had lived it. Now they were using his maps to locate the source of evil that had landed him on this ship in the first place. It had been a while since he had dared to hope that his future wasn't going to just be duty, then death.

Michael turned to the captain and asked, "When will this ship be landing?

"Three days, provided we don't encounter any adverse wind conditions," Miles answered quickly.

Michael thought about the answer a moment before replying, "I want you to change the name of this ship and fly her to Germany."

He looked over at Akio. "Prepare your ship, we're leaving shortly." He turned to the younger paranormals. "Grab your stuff and take it to the ship. Don't leave anything behind."

Mark and Jacqueline left immediately. There were times to ask questions of Michael...

Now wasn't one of those times.

Captain Miles O'Banion stood up and wiped his hands on his pants. "What should the new name of the ship be, sir?"

Michael smiled. "I want you to change it to *Michael the Arch-Angel Returns*," he answered as he walked towards the door. "When you arrive in Germany, this ship is yours to keep, Captain." Michael stopped at the door and looked the captain in the eye.

"What about the original owner?" Miles asked.

"He won't be around to ask about it anymore," Michael replied. "I'll answer the question you had when you first met me, Miles." The captain's shock at being called by his first name was evident as Michael continued, "An honorable vampire *is* as rare as a unicorn. Even rarer actually," he said before stepping into the hallway on his way to his own room to grab his last few items.

\---

"There is no way we are all going to fit inside this ship!" Jacqueline hissed as they walked down the hallway towards the hatch leading to the deck.

"I bet we all fit, and I bet we all make it in one trip," Mark said.

"I don't see it," she replied as she pushed through hatch to the outside.

"Bet you!" Mark closed the hatch behind him.

Jacqueline turned around and pointed at him. Mark stopped suddenly when Jacqueline's finger appeared right in front of his face. "But I'm not doing this for a chore or pushups or some shit. You have to do something real."

"Like?" Mark asked, his eyes crossed as he stared at her finger.

Jacqueline dropped her hand, her eyes narrowing. "You have to paint my nails."

Mark's brow furrowed. "Huh?"

"You know," she waved her fingertips in his face, "fingers, paint. It's decoration."

"I am aware of the existence of fingernail painting, but I've never seen *you* do it."

"That," she answered as she turned around and picked up her bag, "is because we've been living a Neanderthal existence. I've heard that in Europe, people still try to look good."

"Okay," Mark agreed as Jacqueline reached the main hatch.

So damned seductive.

"But if I win, you have to give me a back massage!"

"Guys!" she huffed. "Okay, fine. But you have to find the polish, too."

"Deal!" Mark answered gladly.

Akio turned from the Pod to see the outside hatch open and Jacqueline walk through first, the look of a cunning strategist who had just checkmated her opponent written clearly on her face.

Akio breathed in, then released it.

That poor guy seemed so outclassed.

JAPAN

"YES, AKIO," Yuko answered Akio's question over the video feed. "Eve has reviewed all of the locations. I've tried to pin down the major forces: size and where they are located. The extra protection suits are on their way, and I'll be there later."

"You?" Akio answered, surprised.

"And me!" Eve said from beside Yuko.

Akio, never known for expressions, lost his composure. He stopped talking for a moment, then bowed his head in their direction. "For our Queen."

Both Yuko and Eve bowed back.

ANTIGRAV SHIP *MICHAEL THE ARCHANGEL RETURNS*

THE BLACK POD lifted gracefully off the airship and turned east. It didn't stay at the same height as the blimpy-looking ship, but rose higher into the sky and disappeared. Those on the ship watched it go, and Miles O'Banion stayed quiet a moment.

It was a strange family, and they had arrived by a strange method. Their actions had been stranger yet during the time they were aboard, from their banter to their support and honorable ways. There would be no one beyond his crew who would believe the story should he or his shipmates tell it.

First they would have to believe that Miles wasn't out of his damned mind when he started the story with, "I met an honorable vampire…"

As they stored the luggage in locations that Jacqueline didn't realize were available, she clenched her teeth.

It was obvious that all three of them would not be able to share the one back seat in the craft.

Mark was walking around the Pod, his hands gliding over the wings. The two wings could separate, Akio had told Mark.

"For stability reasons?" Mark had asked the Japanese man.

"No," he replied.

He looked up. "More weapons?"

Akio shrugged. "Perhaps, but I doubt it. The people that built it just happened to like the ship design, and when they could make this one, I believe they did it just because they thought it was, well, 'so fucking cool' is how Bobcat and William said it."

Mark stopped. "Wait, they designed this ship this way because it was cool?"

Akio nodded. "Yes. These ships don't really require a specific shape. We had big rectangular boxes that went to the moon. This is built like an x-wing fighter from a famous movie a long time ago."

Mark looked back at Akio with no recognition on his face.

"*Hai*, I see that I am going to be able to introduce to you the great film *Star Wars*," Akio said as the canopy rose. "In my time, it was considered the same as great literature."

Michael raised his eyebrow as he turned towards them. *Great literature?*

Hai, *many of us in Japan watched it many times*. Akio answered.

I do learn something amazing every day.

What is best, Akio said, *is we have all of the movies, even those I would not wish my enemy to have to watch.*

The Phantom Menace?

This time Akio was shocked silent.

I was awake in the late nineties, Akio.

FRANCE, **Near Paris**

THE LAND WAS dark as the silent black craft drifted down through the clouds to land outside of Paris.

The canopy opened as the ship hovered a foot above the ground. Michael left the ship as Myst and a second later the other three appeared next to it.

Jacqueline sniffed the air. "Not smelling particularly good right now," she told no one in particular. She left to walk up a small hill about a hundred yards away to view the city's remains in the distance. There were lights in some places, and the occasional noise drifted on the wind.

Mark unclasped the door that held their stuff. "Stop," Akio interrupted and Mark looked up, confused.

Akio pointed to the city. "We will leave the gear in the ship for safety."

Mark looked up into the sky. "Yes, up in the air will be safe." Akio said.

"Mark," Michael tilted his head toward Jacqueline. "Safety in numbers." Mark nodded and started off at a jog to where Jacqueline was standing, looking around.

Akio put a hand to his ear and then turned to the southwest. "Eve says we have company coming this way."

Michael sighed. "This place is much more alert than America."

Akio shook his head, his hand still on his ear. "She says it looks like one person in front, being chased by at least twelve more. Speed normal for a human, but those in the rear have elevated heat levels."

Michael turned to the southeast. "Ah, exercise then." He reached into the ship and pulled out his weapons.

Children, come, he commanded, then smirked when he heard Jacqueline's exclamation from the other side of the hill. Her irritation at being called a child didn't stop her from obeying, however.

Mark didn't care one way or another.

Jacqueline's annoyance, written in big bold letters on her face, changed to curiosity and then excitement as Michael tossed her staff to her and a sword to Mark. He pointed towards the southwest. "There's someone being chased. Perhaps human followed by Weres. Ascertain the situation and react appropriately." This time there was nothing but respect as both bowed low.

"Yes, *Sensei*." Jacqueline and Mark turned and started trotting off in the direction Michael had pointed.

"They are good enough for twelve?" Akio asked, no judgment in his question.

Michael slid his coat on, then placed his Jean Dukes in their holsters. "Maybe, maybe not. But they're out of practice. Let's watch them fighting and figure out where they're lacking in skills.

A moment later the black craft's canopy closed and it rose into the darkness. Michael and Akio left quickly and silently in the same direction as the other two.

"Oh my god, oh my god, oh my god!" Sabine ran swiftly, exclaiming between breaths as she made her way towards Paris. She had been walking towards the north when she had encountered the small group of people, and tried to approach their fire.

Until she recognized what was being cooked. Then she had tried to back away, but was unsuccessful.

As soon as the ears, and then heads, swiveled in her direction, she took off. So far, the catcalls from those behind her, and the occasional wolf's howl, let her know that her pursuers were still following.

Playing with her.

Fuck them, she thought. *She could run all damned night if they wanted to keep playing. She wasn't going to quit. They would have to deal with it and force her to go to ground.*

That was when she noticed two people in front of her, coming in her direction.

"Oh my god, oh my god, oh-my-what-the-fucking-shit-is-this?" she gasped and kept running.

She knew what those behind her would do, and she wasn't too keen on being cooked over a flame herself. Perhaps the people ahead of her would kill her, but they might not.

Either way, she kept her legs pumping.

As they came closer, she noticed they had peeled to her left and right and slowed down. Both had weapons, and they had left a space for her to run between them.

So she did.

She sped right through them, yelling, "Run!" She was a good twenty paces away when she glanced back to see that both had stayed in place. "Goddammit!" she hissed and slowed her pace. Finally, she bent over, spitting on the ground with what little saliva she could muster. She straightened up and walked to keep her muscles loose, all the time watching the two newcomers. "I almost did it." She spat again. "Fuck it, I'll slit my own throat." She pulled a knife and was about to jog back to them when she was surprised by another two men who seemed to appear out of the night.

"Put that away," one told her in an Asian-accented voice.

"Watch and learn, little one," said the other. The tall bald man's coat flapped in the breeze as the moonlight reflected off his skull.

"More meat!" Kiandra croaked.

Her pack of twelve growled in their throats when they saw the new two people in front of them. "Seis! Change and grab the girl."

Seis and his mate stopped and stripped, morphing into their wolf forms before they quickly caught up to and then overtook the pack. They worked to get behind the two newcomers, who had turned to see the original quarry being protected by two more men, each with a sword.

Seis howled to let the pack know there was trouble ahead.

Michael moved his sword to his left hand. "One moment, Akio."

Akio looked over to watch Michael pull his coat back and raise his pistol to check the power level. "Seven should be sufficient to slow them down." Michael said, then casually shot both wolves in the head.

Both heads exploded like dropped melons, the bodies flopping end over end in the dirt.

Michael returned the pistol to his holster. "I didn't want to get more blood on me."

"I'm guessing," Mark said as he turned back from watching Michael kill the two wolves, "that Michael has ascertained these are bad people and killing them is an appropriate response."

"Seems like a fair assumption," Jacqueline agreed. "It's like being told there's a pop quiz or something, then being given the answers from the teacher."

"That would have been nice."

"Okay, I'm going to go for double or nothing," Jacqueline said. "I bet I can take out more than you can and if not, I'll double the massage time."

"I don't remember there being a set amount of time in the first place," he replied.

"It was five seconds, since you weren't smart enough to confirm before the bet was placed."

"*Gott Verdammt*," Mark hissed. "What are you anyway, a lawyer?"

"Worse," she replied, her eyes going yellow. "Competitive."

Then she took off running towards the figures in front of them. "You fucking cheater," Mark groused, then smiled. "I like that in my women."

He dashed after her. If he won this bet, that made ten seconds. Then twenty, forty and more than a minute.

He wondered how many of these bets he could win in a row.

The pack slowed down as the two came at them. Four started stripping, two burst out of their clothes and four more pulled their weapons.

It was going to be a free-for-all. Ten against two.

"She seems anxious to get started," Akio opined.

"Oh, she's just trying to get into Mark's pants." Michael said.

"*She* is trying to get into *his* pants?" Akio asked. Michael thought it was amusing that Akio found this surprising.

"Yes, he's a geek and won't figure out she likes him until she knocks him upside the head with a large wooden stick." Michael replied. "Well, larger," he said, "than what she's using at the moment."

"Do we need to get closer?" Akio asked.

"No, these pistols will hit them from here. I want to see how they do together. This should be interesting."

Akio looked sideways at Michael, not sure if the ancient vampire was joking or serious.

9

Mark was getting pissed.

Seriously pissed.

He could read enough emotions to understand that the woman behind them had been running for her life ahead of this pack. She probably didn't expect to stay ahead of the pack forever, but that wasn't going to stop her from trying. Then, in an act of divine providence, she had run into the ArchAngel himself.

Who had told Jacqueline and him to take care of it. He looked at the four humans and six wolves coming at them, and thought about his own recent past.

His hiding who he was, his feeling of loss when the sister he had been trying to nurse back to health had turned on him even though he hadn't touched her.

He had needed her blood to survive, but he had sat by her bed and fed her the soup he had heated up so she could recover from her illness.

Fighting the temptation to drink from her as he nursed her back to health.

He still remembered those men in the alley, the Enforcers,

who had planned to either kill him or strap him down for his blood.

Trapped.

Trapped like this woman, running from those more powerful than her. His growl caused Jacqueline, who was next to him, to glance over in surprise.

She did a double take when she saw how red his eyes were and that his teeth had grown.

"Oh, fuck," she murmured.

She had barely started to yell to Mark to fight with her when he ran towards the ten beings. She took off after him. "*Marrrk!*" she screamed, trying to catch up. "*You fucking lunatic!*"

Mark slammed into the first, a female Were whose eyes glowed yellow. Her mouth stretched and teeth elongated as well, for all the good it did.

He grabbed her head and twisted, slinging the body one way, her skull was still in his hands before he threw it at another attacker. His left-handed punch crushed the second human's face in.

Then a new wolf grabbed his right leg in its teeth and tried to rip it off.

Mark reached down and squeezed the wolf's skull. A small yip was all it got out before its skull popped. Another wolf jumped into the fray, running at full speed to hit Mark in the chest and knock him over. That was when Jacqueline arrived.

"There are no bitches here!" Jacqueline screamed as she shoved her staff through the skull of the second wolf. "Stop laying down on the job, Mark and let's kick some more ass!" she finished, kicking a human in the stomach as she parried a knife slash from her left.

The arm that held the knife disappeared when Mark's sword cleaved it off. "I'll have you know," he replied, "I was just waiting for you to show up, seeing as how you seemed to be admiring all the guys without shirts."

They moved together to fight back to back. "What of it?" she asked. "I noticed you looking at the tits on the girl in the bridge who was ready to..." She stopped talking when one of the humans and two of the wolves hit Mark behind her.

—

"Oh, this is about to get really bloody." Michael commented, watching as the human got a knife into Mark.

"Why?" Akio asked.

"Because she's about to find out just how much of her father she really has in her." Michael replied. "I hope the love that she feels is able to protect her from the curse."

Akio turned back to watch the battle, realizing what he was about to witness.

—

"*Marrrk*!" Jacqueline screamed as her staff slammed into one of the wolves taking down her friend.

Her…

"*You darrrre tooo touccchhh hhhim?*" the guttural voice erupted from her chest as she grew. Her clothes ripping, the woman was replaced by a seven-foot-tall Pricolici. The eyes, yellow with a tinge of red around the edges, announced the death of all who would hurt her Mark.

Her Chosen.

Her Mate.

The man who had stabbed Mark stared in horror as Jacqueline grabbed his arm. He flew over her head as she yanked him off his feet.

But like Mark before her, she kept the arm for herself and used it to beat off a wolf that had tried to attack from her right.

Two wolves chose to flee, turning around to head back to where they came from.

Neither had taken ten steps before their heads exploded in mist, bodies dropping to the ground.

—

Mark looked up in a haze of pain to see the change come over Jacqueline and hear her scream as she announced her proclamation to protect...

Him.

Him!

Never! he promised himself as feelings just about overcame him. Never would another asshat hurt this woman without him by her side. He had turned over on his stomach to get up and back into the fight when her foot shoved him down.

Gently, but firmly.

"I'llll talllk too yoouu innn a mmmooommment," she growled as she worked on the last human still fighting her. He looked up in time to see the claws on Jacqueline's right hand enter the female's chest and rip out her ribs. Then Jacqueline's left hand grabbed the screaming woman by the shoulder and her right shoved back into the chest cavity. She ripped the Were's heart out as she announced, "Yyouuu wonnn't bee neeeeding thiisss annnyyymoorre."

The look of horror on the woman's face was complete as she realized that her heart was in Jacqueline's claws. She dropped to the ground. Jacqueline tossed the bloody heart on top of her and spit on her. "Bitccch, heeeee's minnne."

Both looked around to make sure that everyone was dead before Mark looked up at Jacqueline, who had finally removed her foot. He smiled with his arms open, inviting her to embrace him. "Hey, sweetheart!"

Some distance away, Michael finished holstering his pistol, then turned towards the woman they had saved. "So," he said as he and Akio walked towards her. "Why don't we leave them alone for a little while and get your story, shall we?"

The girl looked at the two men near her and the half-wolf, half-woman in the distance. Her eyes rolled up in her head and she started to collapse into a heap.

"No," Michael told the comatose girl as he jumped forward and caught her before she landed on the ground. "We can't have you hurt yourself while fainting, now."

—

Mark played with Jacqueline's hair. "You know, we should probably find a place to get this blood off you. It's going to be sticky."

Jacqueline pulled her left arm out of Mark's embrace and pointed towards the west. "The ocean is that way."

Mark smiled. "I think it's a little far, plus the salt might not do anything for your hair, baby."

Jacqueline snuggled a little harder into him. "Do that again."

"What?"

"Call me baby."

Mark smiled and just *moved*. Before Jacqueline had realized what was going on, Mark had twisted on the ground and grabbed her as he stood up, cradling her in his arms as he started walking west. "It stinks too much around here to cuddle."

"Mmm hmmm," she replied, placing her arms around his neck. "But you were a badass and I was enjoying your touch too much to care."

"Let's find a lake or some water."

"Whatever you say," she said. Mark walked another fifty paces before he realized she was asleep. He assumed changing into her other form took more energy from her, and he carried her over two more hills before he found a small stream heading down towards the ocean. He gently laid her down next to the water, and for ten minutes he worked to get the blood out of her hair.

It was a damned mess.

But for the first time in Mark's life, it was safe to love someone.

—

"I can take her," Akio suggested, paused, and then completed his sentence, "Michael."

Michael turned to Akio with the young woman in his arms and smiled. "Akio, you're a friend, not a servant. You don't need to hesitate to say my name. You serve the woman I love, and have done so for a hundred and fifty years. I think that qualifies you pretty damned well to call me Michael."

Akio nodded once. "Thank you."

"Now that we have that out of the way." Michael stepped closer to Akio and held out the woman. "Here."

Akio accepted her, but raised an eyebrow. Michael smirked. "This way, if anyone attacks, *I* get to kill them."

Michael thought Akio's soft laugh was one of the most pleasant sounds he had heard in a long damned time.

Now, to move to phase two in his diabolical scheme to make a normal human being out of the vampire.

—

Jacqueline could feel Mark near her, and the effort he was making to clean her hair without pulling it.

He failed miserably. With each little jerk he would miss a few strands, and she was pretty sure there were a billion nanocytes playing tug-of-war with him, both of them yanking for complete control. Not that she cared. She put out a hand, her eyes still closed, and rubbed his leg. "No," she said when he stopped to look at her. "Keep doing that."

She considered her feelings, the fact she had changed into the same form as her father, and her desire to protect Mark. "You need to work more on your fighting."

"Mmm hmmm," he agreed.

"Probably a lot on ground work, too," she grinned. "Lots of us rolling around, sweaty, fighting for control, dominance, submission…" She let her voice trail off.

"Sounds like a good time," he said. "Don't think I'll be that good with a submissive role, but all's fair in love and war."

"Still, going to have to practice, I don't want ever worry about you like that again."

"When do you want to do this?"

Jacqueline's eyes popped open, the yellow flaring as her lips broke into a mischievous grin.

—

Michael turned his head to the right. "Seems like our two young ones are finally consummating their feelings."

Akio just nodded his agreement as he adjusted the young lady. Her eyes were opening and looking up at him.

"Uh," she looked around as the two strange men turned to regard her. "Hello?" she said.

"Can you stand?" Akio asked, his voice soft.

"Can you hold me like this all night?" she replied, a tiny grin on her face.

"Yes," Akio answered truthfully.

She blinked a couple of times. "Oh." She looked around, then closed her eyes and went back to sleep.

Michael chuckled. "I guess she feels safe enough."

Akio shrugged. He tilted his head and said, "Eve, please bring the ship back down." About half a minute later, the black Pod dropped through the night to the ground twenty paces away. Akio took the young woman to the Pod. "Open the canopy." Once the canopy was open, he gently laid her in the back seat and turned to see Michael smiling at him. Akio looked around. "I said I could hold her all night. I didn't say I wanted to. If we get attacked, I'd like to have a little fun as well."

Michael laughed, and soon Akio was laughing himself.

—

Children.

Jacqueline's head lolled on Mark's chest. She was sleeping again after their second go around at wrestling. The second time, he threw her bodily into the water. She was a shit-ton more slippery in the water. Somehow, in all of the strenuous activity in the stream, they had managed to get off most of the blood, but gained a little mud in the process.

Just me at the moment. Mark sent back. *Jacqueline is sleeping.*

Is she tired from changing forms? Michael asked.

Uhhhhh... sure, Mark replied.

There was a flicker of amusement in the connection in response to Mark's answer. *Well, I hope you're not in a compromising position, since you're going to have company in a little while. Yuko and Eve are arriving soon, and have new clothes for both of you.*

Advanced stuff, Akio explained. *Jacqueline's strong desire to protect you caused her to change to Pricolici, so Yuko had to go back to the base for stretchy fabric for when she changes the next time.*

Mark thought about that a second. *Okay. But what about when she goes doggy?* he asked.

A half mile away, Michael winced before replying, *I say this only so that you don't put your foot in your mouth when she is awake. So listen very carefully, Mark.*

Yes?

Do not ever, and I mean ever, call her wolf form doggy. You will regrow your teeth faster than you will be able to find them after she slaps you.

Mark thought about that a moment. *I've got a few things to learn.*

Yes, but welcome to love and all the ups and downs that go with it.

Mark could feel Jacqueline trying to squirm further into his embrace, and he smiled. *Michael, how did you ever figure it all out?*

There was a pause before Michael answered.

Who said I had it all figured out?

10

"AKIO?" EVE'S VOICE RESONATED IN AKIO'S EAR.

"Yes?"

"The biological readings show the young lady in the Pod is waking up."

Akio looked up. "Please bring her down here."

Akio turned to see the Pod descending. As he walked over to it, the canopy was already opening.

The young lady was blinking her eyes open as she stared around the little ship she was sitting inside. "The…" she started, then stopped when Akio walked up. "I thought you were carrying me?" She ran a hand along the side of the chair inside the ship. "I didn't know you were from the future."

"I am from the past, Sabine," Akio replied. "The ship is not from the future. Let me help you out."

"Awwww." She bit her lower lip as Akio reached in and easily lifted her out. "Sorry, but this was the most comfortable and safe I've been in a while."

Akio just nodded.

"Where were you going?" The other man stepped up and Sabine turned. "Hello, my name is Michael."

"Originally?" Sabine replied and pointed behind her. "Paris." She turned to look at the few lights in the distance. "I have a few friends who are holed up in a defensive group inside the city, helping each other from all of the… uh…" She turned to look at the two men. "Others."

Michael smiled. "You mean werewolves and vampires?"

She nodded, believing that she now understood how Akio could hold her all night.

"Do you need to be taken to them?" Akio asked. "We can easily see you safely all the way there."

Her eyes opened wide. "Would you?" she asked. Then she looked confused. "Wait, what about the sun?"

Michael grinned in the moonlight. "What about it?" Her eyes darted back and forth between them. "It won't affect us any more than it does you."

"But," she looked at Akio, who just raised his eyebrows. "I thought you were…"

"Were what?" Michael smirked. "Vampires?"

"Yeah," she admitted. "That seems kind of silly when I think about it. But," she looked over to where the fight had taken place. "I know I saw the girl change into a monster."

Michael pursed his lips and sighed. "No. No, you didn't," he said as he reached to touch both her forehead…

And her mind.

—

Jacqueline yawned and punched Mark softly on the shoulder.

"What's that for?" he asked, his eyes searching the night sky.

"That's for making me think that technology was your first lust."

"It was," he answered.

The slug became real. "Hey!" he exclaimed, giving her his whole attention. "I said it *was* my first, not my last and greatest."

"*Ooohhh*!" She grinned at him and then grabbed his arm to pull him close, looking up to kiss him.

"What was that for, now?" he asked, completely confused by her quick change of attitude.

"For knowing the right thing to say at the right time to make my heart feel better."

Mark blinked at her a few times. "But what if I have the right thoughts, but the wrong words?"

Jacqueline considered his question a moment before answering. "Well, it will suck to be you. Just like every other guy for thousands of years."

Mark wisely stayed quiet. Moments later, they looked up as a large box started descending towards them.

—

Yuko shook her head, a small smile playing on her lips. "Young love. Who would have thought it could blossom around Michael so easily?"

"I doubt even the vaunted ArchAngel could stamp out the attraction of hormones," Eve replied as they ignored the outside monitors once they understood what they had been seeing. "Plus, maybe Michael has changed significantly. He *has* been gone a long time."

Yuko nodded that she understood the statement, but she didn't offer a confirmation that she believed a word Eve was suggesting. Even Eve's own calculations didn't support a significant chance that what she said was true.

But even though the chance was small, the evidence that love was blossoming had been displayed on their screen just a moment ago.

The large container settled on the ground some hundred and fifty paces away, where it was level enough. Eve went to the back and unlocked the doors, then pushed one half open.

Moments later, the two youngsters came jogging up.

Holding hands.

—

Akio nodded as Sabine explained that the group inside the

city would welcome two more warriors gladly. "We'll take you to your friends," Michael said to the young lady, "but first we have a need to do some research on a person who seems to be pulling together packs like the ones who chased you last night."

Sabine's eyes involuntarily darted to the dead bodies and back to Michael. She asked, "You know that there are more like that, yes?"

"Oh?" Michael replied.

She nodded. "Oh yes. I've heard there are at least three large groups. They have camps in some of the small cities around Paris. We're expecting them to attack, and that's why I was trying to make it to my friends.

"You were coming here to fight?" Akio queried.

She turned to answer. "Yes. I lost friends and family last winter to a group that attacked my town. I was on a foray to gather food when it happened." Her eyes glistened as she remembered. "I can't fight much, but I can scout, and I know where three packs are. I can't believe I was stupid enough to believe the ones last night…" She looked around, noticing the false dawn approaching. She shivered. "Well, that they were human."

Michael nodded, getting what he needed from her memories.

"I wish I had weapons and could have killed them myself," she murmured.

Akio pursed his lips, then turned to walk a few steps back to the Pod before reaching in and moving aside two boxes. He pulled out a third, lifting it up and over the side. He brought it back to them before he handed it to her.

Michael raised an eyebrow.

"Here," Akio said as he gave her the box. She grabbed it with both hands, then made a small squeak as she had to grip harder to hold the weight. She lifted it back up.

"What's this?" she asked.

"Two pistols and five hundred rounds of ammunition. We have two hours before we can safely approach your friends. If you truly want to be able to fight back, I will teach you how to fire that weapon and defend yourself."

"But," she looked up at him, "this will only hurt humans."

Akio shook his head "Not anymore. Those bullets are meant to hurt werewolves as well."

"Silver?" she asked, looking down at the box.

"No, better." Akio replied. "It is something a friend created when she was bored. The little tiny machines in the bullets will affect any who attack you."

"Any?" Michael asked.

Akio looked up. "If they have the wrong type of nanocytes, *hai*."

Michael slowly nodded his head. "That's an interesting development."

"It was based on something TOM and Bethany Anne concocted early on. Eve modified it with the instruments in the cave."

"Sabine," Akio said to the young woman, "please be so kind as to make sure you shoot the right people with that. Now," Akio pointed behind her, "let's go use some of those heads as targets."

Waste not, want not. Michael sent to Akio.

It will help her understand how to shoot at people and bodies, more than, say, a tin can, Akio responded.

Michael looked around as they walked back towards the dead bodies. "*Where would you find a tin can out here?*"

—

"Oh my God." Mark looked at the screens. He felt pain in his hand as Jacqueline once again reminded him of his latest *and* greatest love, which was *not* tech.

"Aww, c'mon honey." Mark turned to her. "You have to know that this," he waved a hand at the inside of the container, "can never make me feel as good as you."

She smiled. "Or hurt you as much."

Yuko wanted to roll her eyes at them. "My name is Yuko, and this is Eve."

They looked down at the shorter woman. "I am an android," Eve informed them.

"What's an android?" Jacqueline asked her. "You just look short to me."

Eve turned to her. "I am a sentient AI housed within this fabricated body."

Jacqueline put up two fingers and pointed to her own eyes, before switching the hand around to point the two fingers at Eve. "I found him first, so keep your advanced technology sexiness away from him, understand me?"

—

Michael walked away from Akio and Sabine as he thought about what he knew of the Japanese vampire's skills, and what he thought he understood from his little experiment on the *ArchAngel*.

Where he had argued with the energy of the cosmos, and at least this time, he won.

Another hundred and fifty paces away was a small cluster of trees, so he continued there as he spread his senses to confirm nothing unsafe was around.

Unfortunately, there were only animals keeping their distance, nothing to fight at the moment.

Michael walked up to the first tree, its six-inch trunk stretching a little above his head before the main limbs branched out. There were three branches at eye level. Michael rolled up his sleeve and created a minute cutting edge along his forearm, then used it to cut away the limbs stopping him from easily getting closer.

He kicked away the fallen branches and looked at the wood, wondering if this idea was going to go anywhere.

As near as he could tell, the Etheric was energy. Perhaps raw energy, perhaps something he could manipulate into different forms of energy.

He needed to figure this out, and frankly, he had always enjoyed fires.

When he was fighting the storm, reveling in the power and the pain as the lightning was drawn into his body to be channeled into the Etheric, he had come up with the idea that perhaps he could create fire as he pulled energy—heat—back and forth to try and disturb the clouds.

Michael pursed his lips, trying to remember what he knew. Fire, or at least flame, was the physical manifestation of exothermic reaction when things were heated above their combustion point. Some objects had lower combustion points, some higher.

Wood, at least in the green state, required more than five hundred degrees Fahrenheit to combust, if he remembered correctly. What he couldn't recall was how much more than five hundred.

Michael considered what he was about to do and smiled. He reached up, used the monomolecular edge on his forearm to cut off the branch, caught it, and then cut three, foot-long segments. Taking his three pieces, he walked away from the grove and shook his head.

He might have accidentally started a damned prairie fire if he had tried something inside there. After thirty paces he found a halfway-sandy area and cleared it out. He squatted and placed his first piece of wood in the center of the sand. Staring at it, he willed it to burst into flames.

Nothing happened.

He ran a hand across his head, then shook it. Maybe if he could figure out fire, he could figure out how the hell to grow his hair back. He probably looked like a future version of Yul Brynner, walking around with pistols and a sword.

Thinking a moment, Michael put his hand on the wood and

started to feel for the energy—the core that seemed to be inside him—and tried to place it within the wood. There were no flames, but when he lifted his hand, there were scorch marks where his fingers had held the log.

Michael chewed his lip. His eyebrows drew together in concentration as he placed his hand back on the log, then he deliberately thought of the annoyance he felt about having to wait before he was able to see Bethany Anne again.

The Universe was fucking with him.

That perhaps, just perhaps, she might die before he had a chance to tell her he loved her once more. *Gott Verdammt…*

"*Fuck!*" he said, jumping back from the log that exploded in front of him. Parts were in flame, falling from the sky. He felt a twinge and reached up to his right cheek, where he pulled out the two large splinters that had impaled his face. Looking down, he quickly pulled out another fifteen slivers. He sniffed and turned to his right. Jogging over, he stomped out a small grass fire that had started from a chunk of the log.

Lesson learned. He was touchy about not seeing Bethany Anne again.

Two more logs, two more chances to figure out what might start a fire without exploding the damn material.

—

"This suit," Yuko said, "is made of a very stretchy fabric."

"Can it handle it if I change into a…" Jacqueline stopped and looked at Mark. "How tall was I?"

"Uh," Mark paused a moment. "At least six and a half, maybe seven feet? I was mostly on the ground under your foot, so size was relative at that moment."

Jacqueline blushed. "I… uh, I'm sorry about that." Mark pulled her close as she turned back to Yuko. "If I'm six or seven feet tall?"

"So, you can turn into a Pricolici?" Yuko knew this, but wanted to make sure they spoke about openly.

"Yes."

"The materials can stretch that much, but when you change back, you might have to get it wet and allow it to dry so it will shrink back to the normal size. It could be loose on you until you do."

"Better than walking around buck naked," Jacqueline said.

"Why?" Mark asked. "I'm kinda of fond of..."

"Others?" Jacqueline asked him. "I mean, I'm Were, so I can handle walking around naked in front of a bunch of guys."

Mark turned back to Yuko. "So, do you have another set of these for her? If one gets ripped in a fight or something, we wouldn't want her to be without."

The android came up. "We have plenty. For some reason we are full up on clothes."

"The reason," Yuko turned to look at her friend, "is that you went through a design and creativity phase back in the fifth decade, but didn't have enough people to use them."

"Not my fault that Japan went all insular again," Eve argued.

"My people have *always* been a bit insular," Yuko replied. "It is close to what 'Japanese' means in most languages."

Eve just shrugged.

SABINE AIMED THE PISTOL AND...

"Don't," Akio told her. "Don't aim the gun, make it an extension of your thoughts, of your being. It isn't there to be aimed. It is there to send the bullet where your mind wishes it to go." He held a hand out. "Let me have one."

Sabine gladly handed the pistol over. "You forgot to take it off safe," he said. He glanced at the bodies and heads. Some were close, others were farther away. Sabine watched him. His body was facing her, but his gaze was downrange before he turned back to look at her. "Each." He fired a shot; it split a head in two. "Time." He fired again, still looking at her. She saw a body twitch about thirty paces from the skull he had shot first. "You shoot." Another squeeze of the trigger, another hit. "You just feel the bullet and the target become one, and will your body to make it happen."

She saw his next three shots hit bodies farther away. Her mouth dropped open. "You didn't even look!"

He shook his head. "I did look," he said. "Then, it is in here," he touched his head with his left hand. "and here." His hand dropped to his chest over his heart. "A gun is a tool to make your will a reality when someone attacks you and your people. A tool for protection."

Her mind was leagues away before his voice cut through her memories. "Sabine?"

Her head jerked around. "Sorry!" She flashed him a short smile. "I'm sorry. you mentioned protection." Akio nodded. "I'm still thinking of my parents, my friends, and their senseless deaths."

"That is good, Sabine. If you are going to take a life, you must have a reason to do so. The protection of your friends' lives is a better motive than revenge, but justice for the dead is a very close second. I will share a few tricks with you that I have learned over the years," he said as he flicked the pistol's safety back on.

She accepted the weapon, verifying that the safety was on before reloading, as he had taught her. "How many years is that?"

"More than you can guess, little one," he whispered.

Moments later, both pistols loaded and safeties off, Sabine stood ready. "You will walk forward, Sabine. Each time I call out, you will shoot to either your left or right, whichever has a closer target. But you will not be thinking of them as targets; you will be thinking and believing they are alive. They are the ones attacking your village."

Sabine nodded her understanding.

"Now, I want you to be ready, and I want you to walk straight and look straight, even if the target is off to your side. Do you understand what I am telling you?"

"Look straight, walk straight, shoot wherever I need to," she replied.

Akio nodded as he insinuated himself into her mind. He tapped the memories she had pushed down, but still used to fuel her anger.

Her drive.

Walk, and let us kill those who attack the people you love.

—

The memories came back, but this time she could smell the smoke, hear the screams, and feel the wind blow across her skin.

Her breath caught in her throat.

You have the power to protect them, little one, the voice told her. She looked down to see the two pistols in her hands.

How did you two get here?

She took a step. *Your future is ahead of you. Protect, or die, Sabine.*

The buck of the first pistol in her grip barely registered. She stared ahead, aware of those who were attacking as she continued. She barely heard the commands to fire, then she lost even that guide as she felt the pain of those who were dying, the fear as children were murdered, their arms ripped off by the teeth of creatures that should not exist.

Those that were not killed by the people of her village. A creature went down each time her pistol bucked in her hand, and the ones she shot didn't get back up.

Her right pistol shot twice, then her left once, and she continued walking forward. She looked into the distance, unseeing but uncannily accurate.

Turn around, five shots, duck!

Sabine spun, fired and ducked.

Left, left, right, left, right!

Back to the front!

She continued her twist and stood back up. She yelled into the morning light, "Bring it, assholes!"

In ten more steps, her guns went silent.

The enemies from her past all lay dead behind her.

She was coming back into her own mind when she heard the warning. "*Attack above you!*"

Both pistols whipped up as she turned around and found two pieces of wood flying towards her head.

Blam blam!

The pistols barked in her hands and both branches exploded into splinters.

"*Safety!*" came the command, and Sabine easily flipped them both on.

She looked towards Akio, who wore a small smile as he waved her towards him. He turned, and she watched him head toward the ship. She walked past the targets and was able to see where all the shots had hit.

All but two were close to dead center. One was high and to the right, the other barely clipped. She noticed the five shots she had made as she turned around. All five were on target, but not dead center.

She would have to feel for the target harder next time.

Akio was returning from the ship when she finished walking past the bodies on the ground. They smelled horrible, but she had smelled that odor before.

He was carrying a belt. "Here are holsters for your weapons." She reached out and he shook his head. "No. I will put this on you the first time. Then, until you die, you will be the only one to don or remove these weapons. Is this understood?"

Sabine nodded and lifted her arms as Akio put the belt around her and cinched it up. He adjusted it so the holsters hung correctly on her hips. "It is time," he said.

She lowered her hands and placed each pistol in its holster. As she settled the second pistol, she looked at Akio. "Thank you."

He offered a half smile to her, then turned to look into the distance. Sabine wasn't sure why, so she twisted to see what he was gazing at.

There were four people walking towards them. The two on the left were holding hands.

"Sabine," Akio introduced everyone as they walked up. "The young man on the left is Mark, and those are Jacqueline and Yuko. The short one is Eve."

Sabine nodded to each in turn.

"Where's Michael?" Jacqueline asked.

Akio turned towards the north.

Michael?

Are you done, gunslinger? Michael asked, joy coloring his speech.

I am done for now, Akio agreed.

Good. Everyone but Sabine noticed the piece of wood that shot up into the sky above the hill, but even she noticed when it exploded in flame.

I'm in need of some more fun.

—

The building was made of cement. Its windows were up high, and the morning sun was starting to stream through them. A middle-aged man walked through the double doors, a rifle held casually over his shoulder. "They're coming, Kirk," he called. His walk was neither fast nor slow.

The rusty-brown haired, bearded man looking over the maps on the table called back, "Which ones, James?"

"The Yellows," James replied as he arrived at the table. "From the west. Early reports give us maybe an hour, hour and a half tops."

Kirk nodded and moved an old bolt he had painted yellow closer to the city. "So it begins." He tapped the table twice. "I wonder how the Yellows were chosen as the first pack to come after us?" They had named all the packs by color to distinguish them.

James shrugged. "Not sure it matters, but it's something that will forever bug the hell out of me now that you've planted the question in my mind."

Kirk smiled grimly. "Are the teams in place?"

His friend and second nodded. "In place, or heading there. It's just you, me, and the six who stay with us."

Kirk nodded. "We have the snipers?"

James scratched his chin. "Yes, and they have some balls to be out there, willing to take those early shots without protection from the others."

Kirk shrugged. "We all have an appointed time to die." He reached down to a chair on his left and grabbed a vest. It had many sewn loops with cartridges in them.

Large cartridges.

Turning to his right, he grabbed a sawed-off shotgun. "Let's go out like the heroes we are."

—

Adorjan was running free with his tongue hanging out of his mouth, a howl ready in his throat. There were five hundred fifty-three Weres strung out behind him. He had been ordered to take out the groups of humans in Paris so that his master could finally subjugate the once-amazing city. Over the last decades, he and his pack had first silently, then not-so-silently attacked the humans after the Duke had taken control.

And taken control he had. Quickly and decisively. Adorjan had been third in the pack when the Duke ruthlessly and efficiently took out the Alpha and his second. Adorjan had taken all of five seconds to decide the Duke was an acceptable Alpha for him. The news had come this morning that the Duke expected to be able to enter Paris without problems in just a few days, should he want to.

The silhouette of the old city skyline was lighting up, the early morning sun reflecting from panes of glass still in the windows after so many years.

Paris would be the Duke's.

—

"We have a large contingent of Weres approaching from the city north of us," Eve said.

"Send a puck to disrupt their flow, Akio," Michael said.

Akio turned to look at Yuko and raised an eyebrow.

"Yes, three are available," Eve said.

Michael turned to look at her. "You only have three?"

"It has been a very action-heavy hundred and fifty years, Michael-*san*." Yuko replied. "We are making more, but we have only three with us at this time."

"The technology we have," Eve added. "It is the ability to make some of the parts we lack. We are slow to build them."

"There was a large fight in China some five months ago," Akio continued the explanation. "The only way to deal with them, I felt, was to pummel the location with pucks."

"And by pummel," Yuko interjected, "he means bomb them until nothing was standing."

"What kind of enemy was this?" Michael asked.

"Chinese Weres in the jungle." Akio replied. "They preferred to stay there instead of engaging in a straight-up fight."

Michael smiled. "Okay, if three is all we have, then let's send one right into the middle of them, or inside the biggest group between the center of the pack and the first wolf."

"Why not just bomb the Alpha?" Jacqueline asked.

"These are going to be under the control of the Duke, I'm sure," Michael said. "There are already instructions in place and whether they have an Alpha or not, they will complete the mission." Michael looked around. "Let's grab a ride and see if we can make a difference."

—

Sabine was strapped into one of the drop seats in the container that Yuko was using to transfer the materials Akio had requested. Michael had one of the two doors on the end open. He clutched a handhold and was looking out of the door.

She averted her eyes and looked at Jacqueline, who was answering a question. "No, we came from America."

Sabine forgot the uneasiness in her stomach. "Really?"

Mark nodded. "Yes, we were on a ship on the way here when Akio picked us up, and then we landed in front of you last night."

"That was an accident?" Sabine asked, remembering her panicked run. They had shared food with her, which had helped her stomach and given her energy as well. No one had asked if she wanted to stay behind. Sabine looked over to see Akio talking with Yuko and Eve.

—

"Yes, I will be a part of this!" Yuko hissed, her eyes fiery with anger.

"You have stayed out of most of the fighting for a hundred and fifty years, Yuko," he observed. "What is causing this strong desire to be a part of it now?"

Yuko clamped down on her first response. With her left hand, she reached out and covered Eve's mouth.

Akio raised an eyebrow and Yuko shrugged. "Eve is always guessing out loud. I want to answer this myself." Yuko thought for another couple of moments. "It is time that I carried some of the load," she said finally. "I was charged, just as you were, to await Michael's safe return to Bethany Anne and to do that, my role was as the diplomat." Her eyes flashed red once as she looked out into the space beyond them.

Akio stayed out of her mind. He had promised he wouldn't ever read her unless it was a life or death situation, and it hadn't reached that level.

Yet.

His own eyes narrowed as he realized what was pushing her buttons. Yuko, for as long as he had known her, was the biggest romantic he had ever met. Her belief in the power of love and her wish to see it blossom and create happiness were the reasons she opened her eyes every morning, he was sure.

Why she was so unlucky in her own love, he never understood.

Yuko was shocked a moment later when her taciturn friend reached out and pulled her into a hug. Her eyes, round with surprise, looked over at Eve, whose own expression was disbelief. Eve shook her head slightly.

"I got nothing!" she whispered.

Michael was busy looking out the door, a small smile playing at the edges of his own lips. *Yes, keep her there for a few moments. This is the way you center your friends, Akio.*

This is strange, Michael, Akio replied, his mental voice halting.

Welcome to the opposite of killing your way to answers.

Akio felt Yuko's body lose some of its rigidity, and she hugged him back.

"Stay behind me, little one," Akio whispered to his friend. "I am responsible to the Queen for you as well. She wants you back."

She nodded into his shoulder. "I have your back, old man," Yuko replied, a small tear running down her cheek. "Sorry, old *wise* man."

Akio chuckled.

Once.

When they separated, Yuko reached up and put a hand on Akio's arm. "You taught me to dance, as well. I will not embarrass you." Akio nodded his understanding and watched as she untied the front of the pretty robe she was wearing. Jacqueline and Sabine watched as she took it off.

Yuko wasn't paying attention when the two women's jaws dropped as she stood there in polished, black form-fitting armor. She folded her robe and grabbed two swords, inserting them into her hip sheaths. Then she grabbed a set of shoulder holsters and slid her arms through the openings. The butt of the guns lay along her ribs, and she clipped the tiedowns to her belt to hold them in place.

Michael's voice was gentle, if firm, when she turned around. "Bethany Anne would approve of your clothing choices." She smiled when he winked at her. "Now," he continued as he looked across the weapons laid out along the wall, "let's see if you have something a bit stouter than this Wakizashi, hmm?"

"Oh!" Mark jumped in. "We can go shopping for weapons now?"

Yuko looked him up and down. "First armor, then weapons."

1 2

In the last one hundred and fifty years Akio had yet to meet anyone who could best him in hand-to-hand combat. At one level that had been satisfying, but on another level it meant he didn't know what he could achieve.

Now, as the container they were riding in slowly started to descend, he took a moment to look at Michael. Really *look* at him, and size him up.

His stance, his graceful way of moving. A tic by his eye was the only sign that he was annoyed with himself.

If he hadn't known who Michael was, he wouldn't have guessed him to be so deadly, which meant Akio had a blind spot.

It wasn't that Michael didn't have a certain fluidity to his movements, but he didn't announce his abilities with every move, every decision.

Michael's eyes would crinkle in amusement at times. Usually it would stay there unless he touched his head. It was obvious that his lack of hair was bothering him. Even that annoyance went away quickly though, when something else caught his attention.

He had a certain boyish charm to his manner, to be sure. But when he was angered or felt slighted, the person Akio had heard described in the past came out.

The Patriarch was just under the skin, waiting to take over. Michael wore his easy-going personality like a new set of clothes. He was trying to grow into the man they represented, but his old clothes fought to stay relevant.

Akio didn't give the old clothes much of a thought. Bethany Anne would see that they were tossed out eventually. "Akio?" He turned to see Yuko unlatch the bottom shelf that held the sword Bethany Anne had given him. He nodded to her, and she pulled it out and lifted it to offer it to him.

He hadn't used it in a long time, mostly because he felt it needed to be a special occasion. Right now, his first battle by Michael's side would be just such an occasion.

Yuko approached him, a sense of peace emanating from her as she held it with two hands. "Our Queen provided this sword for your use. It seems fitting that it should go into battle by Michael's side." Akio turned and found Michael smiling at him. It took only a half second before Michael shook his head.

"Oh, no," Michael told him. "Bethany Anne would have a fit if I accepted the sword from you. She gave it to a Queen's Bitch. That Queen's Bitch needs to be the one to use it for her."

Akio's lips tried on a size-two smile, something just a bit bigger than he would normally show. The muscles in his face screamed in agony, as they weren't used to the man stretching them to smile. His frowning muscles, however, were in top shape. *Good thing the nanocytes in my body helped overcome the challenge*, he thought.

"*Hai!*" he agreed, and accepted the sword from Yuko.

—

"What the hell is that?" James asked, as he pointed to the sky to their left. They were all standing on top of a tall building, waiting for the pack to reach them.

"The hell…" Kirk wondered.

"It's a box," Timothy answered from behind them, a scope to his eye. "And get this—there's a man in it looking out an open door." He pulled the gun away from his eye. "Want me to take him out?"

"The Duke?" James asked.

Kirk shook his head. "No, if the Duke is truly a vampire, he can't be in the sun and this guy certainly is."

With the rifle up to his eye, Timothy spoke again. "He seems to be looking down at the werewolves and pointing at something."

Timothy yanked the gun from his shoulder. "What happened?" James asked, noticing that Timothy seemed spooked.

"Uh…" Timothy turned to look towards the dust billowing where the Yellow pack was flowing towards them from the west. "I get the impression he didn't appreciate me aiming my rifle at him."

"Okay," Kirk said, perplexed. "I'll bite. How would he even know you were aiming at him? He's too far away."

"Apparently not." Timothy shook his head. "Might seem weird to you, and certainly seems weird to me, but I'd put my hand on my grandmother's grave and swear that he just told me to aim my rifle somewhere else or he would come over here and shove it up my ass."

All seven men on the roof turned to look at Timothy, who held the rifle in one hand, and put the other up. "This hand will swear right here."

The men all had a good laugh as they turned to the west when they felt, more than heard, a deep sound and saw a large eruption of dirt from the direction of the wolves.

"Now what the hell?" Kirk asked.

Timothy put the scope up to his eye and looked. "Kirk, you ain't going to believe this shit, but it's raining wolves out there."

—

Adorjan barked twice and stopped running. He turned

around to witness something he never expected to see: his pack falling from the sky along with massive amounts of dirt and rocks. He heard two yips from his left where one of his wolves was hit by falling debris.

The humans had used a bomb on his pack.

His pack!

His eyes glowed a deeper yellow as he howled commands for them to catch up. The wounded would have to heal on their own. His anger was all-consuming. Now he didn't want to taste the death of these humans because he had been ordered to, he wanted their blood all over his teeth because they dared to hurt his people.

As the stragglers made it to the larger group, he changed and stood in his large human form. "They dared to bomb our people!" He turned and faced the city where many of them could make out tiny flickers of movement. "Leave not a one alive!" Adorjan changed back to a large sand-colored wolf and howled his anger as he bolted towards the city.

That's when he saw the flying box take off into the sky. There was a new group of humans between his pack and the city. More to rip and tear before they reached the main concentration.

That worked for him just fine.

—

The men watched as the wolves stopped to regroup. The floating container lowered itself to a large swath of ground between the city proper and the wolves advancing on them.

When the container left, there were seven people on the ground.

Kirk could hear noises from Timothy's rifle, and turned to see him sliding the scope off. "What?" he asked. "Your sights are gonna be all sorts of fucked up now."

"Yeah, maybe," Timothy agreed as he put the scope up to his eye. "But I don't have to worry about shitting out the barrel of my gun an inch at a time either," he said. "We got one weird-ass group out there, boss."

"Here, let me see," Kirk ordered, and Timothy passed the scope over to him. He put it up to his eye, then pulled it down and used his shirt to clean it

—

"What are they doing?" James asked as he watched Kirk look at the people in the distance through Timothy's scope. "Kind of a motley crew."

"The Motley Seven?" Kirk snorted.

"Just answer my question. You're hogging the scope."

"Looks like they're dressing their line." Kirk responded.

"What line?" James asked in confusion. "There are only seven of them."

"James?" Kirk asked. "What does your cousin look like?"

"Gracie?" James responded. "You can't miss her, redhead and skin white enough to blind you on a full moon night."

"No," Kirk snorted, "not Gracie."

"Sabine?" James tried a second time.

"Yes."

"Well, when she was alive, she had black hair."

"Uh huh," Kirk replied. After a moment, he gestured. "Keep going."

"Blue eyes, thin. She was a runner."

"No," Kirk told him as he turned and handed him the scope. "It's not 'was.'"

"What?" James grabbed the scope from his friend and put it up to his eye. "The hell?"

"That's my line," Kirk said.

"She's got guns," James blurted. "She... *She's alive?*"

"And she along with six others are about to take on five hundred Werewolves."

"That's not a motley crew, guys," Timothy said. He had taken the scope from James and was looking through it. "Whoever those two older men are, they're killers."

"How can you tell?" Kirk asked.

"Because they wear their weapons like extensions of themselves."

James smiled. "Fuck it! I'm going down."

They whooped in delight as Kirk called over the old radios, "All hands, do not fire. Eagle's Nest is coming down and joining the Magnificent Seven."

"Michael," Akio stated, "you are in the middle, with Jacqueline, Mark and Eve to your right. Sabine, Yuko and myself are to your left."

Michael raised an eyebrow. "Eve?" He looked over at the tiny woman, who smiled up at him.

"It took me three decades to come to the conclusion that killing wasn't against my protocols," she told him.

Michael glanced over to Akio before returning to Eve. "Protocols?"

"She had to figure it out for herself," Yuko said as she checked her pistols. She had a sword on her back, but wasn't planning on using it. "She had a dump of ADAM's programming, including a special section that he didn't tell anyone he had included. She had to find it out for herself, let me tell you." Yuko pulled both pistols and shot four times with each hand.

Seven wolves dropped in the distance, and were dodged by their packmates. None of them realized that their friends were not getting back up.

"Damn, I missed one." She chewed on her lip. "Okay, that *is* upsetting."

Akio looked at Michael. "She's ready."

"Why," Mark asked, looking over at Jacqueline, "do I feel superfluous?"

"Probably because you two and Akio are our close support,"

said Michael. He nodded to the wolves. "When they get up here, it's going to be a melee. Make sure you protect Sabine."

"Hello the group!" a voice called out behind them. They turned around.

"James?" Sabine said softly.

"Know him?" Akio asked.

Sabine nodded. "He's my cousin. He's the one I was coming to see."

"Seems like it's family reunion time now." Michael smiled. "New plan, make sure your friends don't fire on those trying to help them."

Sabine looked over at him and Michael answered her unspoken question. "Not all things that go bump in the night are afraid of the sun, Sabine."

The woman turned to stare at Jacqueline, who looked at her and smiled as her eyes flashed yellow. "Oh. Ohhhh."

You are the wind, Akio's voice rippled through her mind and she nodded her understanding to Michael.

—

The humans were spreading out. A bald man in a coat stood in the middle of the group. Adorjan aimed at him, as any Alpha would.

Challenge accepted.

There were more humans behind the first ones; all of them had weapons. What this pitiful group expected to accomplish against his pack of five hundred Weres, Adorjan wasn't sure.

It was obvious that humans had learned of the paranormal and these people had found enough silver to kill his pack members that had tried to infiltrate the city.

That was one of the reasons the Duke had held off attacking so far.

Occasionally the Duke would send his son and that group of useless vampires into the city to foment more fear. It worked, to a point. What it also accomplished was offering the humans a way to figure out how to take down vampires, with all the practice they were given.

Garlic was useless; crosses were laughed at. Massive amounts of damage and burning solved the vampire problem just fine, though. Vampires, or Weres for that matter, were able to heal their injuries. However, if someone did enough damage it would overcome that ability and they would die.

Five hundred against fifteen and whatever number of humans were behind them?

His pack would be feasting on the bones before lunchtime.

"Sabine!" hissed James from behind her.

"Yes?" she answered, calmly looking out over the werewolves they could see amassing against them. The snipers behind them were firing downrange.

The fight would begin soon.

"You know how to use those things?" James asked, not understanding how his cousin was both alive and wearing pistols he didn't recognize. The pistols were modified, for sure. She had some special cartridges that seemed to plug into the grips of the pistols, a total of six stored along the back of her belt.

Timothy, next to James, whistled. "Nice cartridges," he said, and turned to wink at James.

"Tim, that's my cousin!" he hissed back. "Don't make the first person I shoot be you!"

"No, I'm good with you shooting Tim," Kirk jumped in. "That's just one less for me to worry about, and you don't count. You're her cousin."

Yuko looked over at Sabine, who was rolling her eyes. "Are they fighting over you?"

Sabine looked back at the Japanese woman. "Last night I was running away from werewolves, now I feel like running towards them because of these jackasses behind us."

Yuko shrugged. "It's kinda cute, in a barbaric sort of way."

"Barbaric?" Kirk responded.

Michael snorted from the other side of Yuko. "Watch the outside, people. Gunslingers, let's start." He put action to words and Kirk's eyes about bugged out when the bald man threw back the sides of his coat and grabbed two pistols, then started punching holes in wolves some distance away.

Just what the hell were those pistols?

"Oh, holy fuck…" James whispered as fountains of gore exploded. He couldn't quite make out what the hell was happening, but he could see the results.

"The hell…" Timothy said.

"That's my line!" Kirk argued.

—

Yuko winked at Sabine. "I've got longer range, so be patient, young one."

Young one? Sabine thought. *How old are you?* That's when she noticed the delicate Japanese woman's eyes flash red as she unholstered her two pistols.

"The thing about fighting just anyone," Yuko stated as she raised her pistols, "is that you never know who was blessed to have met Jean Dukes in their past."

Akio nodded in appreciation as Yuko started slamming rounds into the wolf pack. Yuko's face showed no distaste for her kills. He wondered what was going through her mind just then.

The wolf pack was now only a quarter mile away. Akio unholstered his pistol and started shooting randomly. He decided that he didn't want to only be close-in support.

Yuko was humming to herself, an ancient song she sang when she wanted to lose herself.

Michael started walking forward, both pistols continuing to fire.

Behind them, the men looked at each other, eyes wide in amazement. "The hell are these people?" Kirk whispered to James.

From in front of them, Michael answered his question. "We are the Magnificent Seven." He and the one called Akio laughed at their joke.

Kirk, Timothy and James swallowed.

Had they heard them?

Inside Paris

"We will head out tonight," the Duke said to Gerard, "and take out any remaining humans. If the Rehbolson Pack is unsuccessful by midmorning, send in the rest on my command. I wish to have Paris in my control before I go out at midnight, is that understood?"

His butler merely bowed and turned to leave as his master went into his secured room to sleep.

Tonight he would be the second most powerful man in Europe, and the most powerful human.

The other humans just didn't know it yet. First Paris, then old France, and then Germany would fall, and eventually there would only be one trusted human running the empire during the day.

And only one trusted to get close enough to the Duke to help him sleep a final time, making the assassin the *most* powerful man in all of Europe.

The blood the Duke had shared with him already provided him with a superior body; he didn't need hundreds of years to enjoy himself before someone else had the crown.

But he wanted enough years to make all of his slaving for the Duke worth it.

13

Adorjan could hear cries of pain coming from behind him as he maintained his relentless pace, heading for the humans who were not only shooting but killing his pack.

He would have to be deaf not to hear the sounds of his pack exploding behind him. He wasn't sure how that had happened, but the people in front of them must have obtained weapons from before WWDE. When they killed them, Adorjan would keep the weapons for himself and perhaps, just perhaps, he might kill the Duke with them.

Wouldn't *that* make all of these deaths around him worthwhile?

Those human bastards were actually walking towards his people, not running in fright as they should be. His growls and howls of anger were answered by those around him.

One hundred yards left.

—

"So, do I get to have some fun, or do I have to stay like this?" Jacqueline asked, the desire to change already feeding into her system.

Mark looked from his love to Michael, who was still shooting and muttering little adages. "Like shooting fish in a barrel" was one of his favorites.

Michael turned to the humans behind them. "If any of you dare shoot us in the back, I will personally rip your arm off and shove it up your ass."

Sabine turned around and added, "Right before I shoot you myself. Don't fuck with my friends."

Everyone noticed that the two of them still aimed and fired while talking to them.

"The hell?" said two of the guys behind Kirk, James and Timothy as Michael and Sabine turned back around. Kirk sighed.

Then Michael holstered his weapon.

"Wait for it!" he commanded. "Yes, that means you, Jacqueline!" he added to the young woman.

—

"Did her eyes just flash yellow?" James asked no one in particular.

Sabine's head whipped around. "Don't make me shoot you, James!"

James shook his head. "You know?"

Sabine nodded. "You got my back, cousin?" she asked.

"I had guessed," Kirk joined the conversation. "There's always a Yin and Yang to everything. But what about the short one?" he asked, looking at Eve.

Eve turned to regard the young man. "I am an Artificial Intelligence, created by the first of my kind, ADAM out in space, and sent here to keep my friends sane as they accomplished their task to be ready when the ArchAngel came back. They are to keep him safe until the Queen returns. In the decades since, I have achieved my own sentience and powers." She lifted a hand. It had a gun with a square barrel, two inches on a side, and a bunch of small holes in it.

She turned back and aimed towards the right, where wolves were trying to flank them. "While I am not a supporter of indiscriminate killing, I have found some who really do justify termination."

With that, Eve lifted her right leg and slammed it into the dirt. Once, twice, thrice. "You need a good brace to fire this fucker," she added. "It's a new design using some of the Jean Dukes technology to get them going, then rockets kick in to guide to the targets." She leaned forward and squeezed the trigger. The little woman was tossed backwards as she yelled, *"Wheeeee!"* and slammed into Alan, who had been five feet behind her. He tried to catch her but was barely able to slow her down when the suddenly active android hit him. They continued to fly back another five feet before landing with a thump.

A hundred yards away, twenty-five wolves exploded in gore. Behind him, Kirk could hear the little android apologizing to Alan with, "Wow, more kick than I had realized, fucker went to fifteen."

Yuko snorted from up front.

"Akio?" Michael called out. "Care to dance?"

"Always, Master Michael," Akio agreed and holstered his pistols.

Sabine took a moment to slam her last two cartridges into her guns. She looked back at the guys she had come to join. "It's time to get behind us!"

Kirk and James stared at each other. "You sure this is your cousin?" Kirk hissed to his friend, who shrugged his shoulders and nodded.

Akio's amusement could be seen in his eyes as he moved towards Michael.

He was sure this dance would be one of the best of his life.

He wasn't disappointed.

Michael spoke as the pack was crossing the final hundred

yards. By agreement, no one had shot the Alpha yet. Michael's eyes flashed red. "The interesting thing about packs is that any time you take out the Alpha," Michael shot his hand up, "it causes confusion. In battle, confusion is thine enemy."

—

Adorjan, his focus on the bald man in the middle, was one of the first to know without a doubt that he was running straight towards his worst nightmare. The red eyes gave the man away; that he was in the sun provided the second most important clue as to how powerful a vampire he was streaking towards.

As his skin and hair were engulfed in flames, he had no doubt which of the myths from the vampires' past he had just been running towards.

"Michael…" was his last thought as his blood began to boil.

—

"Son of a bitch," James whispered as the Alpha of the wolf pack in front of them was consumed in flames. The wolf lasted another three leaps before he exploded, raining chunks of burnt flesh and fire across the other members of the pack.

Many had lost their will to fight but were being pushed forward by those who came behind them—those who had not yet seen what their Alpha had recognized just before he died.

Two of them figured that it would be better to see if they could go to ground and hope their pack missed them. They split to the side rather than face the death they knew was waiting for them in front.

One died, trampled by his pack. The other broke out, one leg shattered and one ear gone, but alive.

In the middle, the dance of the two swordmasters was beautiful to watch. Michael had exchanged the wakizashi for an Ulfberht. He took the head of a wolf to his right as he kicked the one coming straight at him in the chest and knocked it back. You know," Michael said casually, "I never understood why everyone always believes the katana is superior to a European sword." Michael swung his left arm back, forming a serrated Etheric edge around his hand as he stabbed into the chest cavity of a wolf that had tried to duck and come under the one Michael had kicked back.

"It started with the movies," Akio replied. He brought his own katana down, slicing a wolf's head in two from the top of the skull through its jaws. Another wolf was preparing to jump over his kill when its head exploded in gore.

Yuko was on the job.

"Then," Akio continued his turn and ran a wolf through its chest, "those that loved the romanticism of the katana continued with Anime and Manga." Akio pulled his sword clear, then pivoted on his right foot and swept his sword low to amputate two legs from the nearest wolf. When Michael reached across to slash a wolf through the back, Akio turned again and moved across to Michael's unprotected side to remove the jaw of another one that was seeking to hamstring Michael.

"Well," Michael said, not worrying about any area Akio had under control, "the Vikings themselves forged crucible steel." He brought his sword around his shoulders and swung it up from the ground. The wolf that was jumping towards him received a slice in the chest and a boost that sent it flying over Michael's head.

He heard a shotgun blast, which he figured was from the one called Kirk.

—

"Are you fucking kidding me?" Mark asked, annoyed.

"They really don't want to give anyone a chance to get a sword or club in edgewise, do they?" Jacqueline replied.

"Over here!" Eve called for their attention as ten new wolves circled the large group that was trying to get to the man they thought had killed their Alpha.

"About damned time!" Jacqueline threw down her staff.

"Uh oh," Mark said. "Honey?"

"Don't honey me!" Jacqueline hissed. "I'm done playing second fiddle and waiting for werewolf scraps!"

"Oh, for fuck's sake!" Mark huffed out. "Fine! But you better keep your foot off me or I'll bite it!"

Eve looked around at Alan, who was standing behind her, and shrugged her shoulders. The little AI turned again and took a step back as Jacqueline howled her challenge.

—

"Oh my god!" Alan retreated from the new monster in front of him, and involuntarily raised his weapon when a bullet whizzed by.

He jerked his head around to see Sabine looking at him over her pistol's sights. "Don't make me put it closer next time!" she said.

"Sorry!" he called back. "Just took me by surprise."

"You aren't the only one," Kirk agreed. James had his shotgun barrel in his hand, which had kept Kirk from aiming at the new monster.

Sabine turned back around and started shooting.

Left, left, right, right, left.

You are doing well, gunslinger, his voice said in her mind, and Sabine smiled.

—

Of the ten Weres that had circled the larger group, the grey female in the front was the hungriest. Bernase was a strong supporter of Adorjan, and had tried on multiple occasions to get him to commit to a relationship with her. But every time she thought she had a chance, another female would intrude and she went back to living in obscurity again. Now Adorjan was dead, and these people had killed her dreams. While many of her pack-mates were busy trying to get at the leader, the Alpha of the human pack, she and those following her would kill the others on the edge.

She was eyeing the young woman—not the short one, she didn't smell right—when the human threw down her pole in anger. Bernase wasn't against a foe who acted stupid, and this would only make her easier to kill. That's when the girl changed into a form from her kind's own mythology.

Bernase was about to attack a Pricolici. It took her only another second to realize that the man next to her was a day-walking vampire. Bernase lasted long enough to know she was about to join Adorjan before the standing Pricolici grabbed her head in a vice-like grip and squeezed.

Inside Paris

GERARD USED powerful binoculars to view the skirmishes in the distance, and what he saw was most annoying.

Not only was the pack that was supposed to be attacking not yet in the city, but from what little he could tell, it looked like the fight was going against them.

Hard to believe, but he had to work with what he could see, and he saw that the Weres had failed.

He took off his backpack and placed it on a hook on the half wall that was still standing upright on the seventh-floor landing. Reaching into the left side of the pack, he pulled out a small transceiver and clicked the buttons twice and three times, then twice and four times in a predetermined signal.

He repeated the pattern until he heard a long beep, then two beeps and one long one.

Gerard placed the transceiver back in his bag. He looked back to the west and shook his head. It was annoying that they would have to bring all of the local packs into this battle. The cleanup was going to be a mess, and the sharing of spoils had just gotten more complicated.

Weres could be such a pain in the ass when loot was to be distributed. However, it wasn't his job to deal with issues, that was up to the Duke.

His job was to make sure the city was subdued for his boss when he woke up later this evening. Now at least another two thousand Weres were on their way. They should be here right after lunch.

—

Blam! Kirk racked another shell into the chamber, then the slug from his shotgun blew the Were who was trying to get a bead on James in half. His rounds weren't silver, but when you caused enough damage, the job got done.

Then a single bullet went into the Were's brain, and the lights slowly went out.

Kirk turned around to see Sabine aiming to her left, her right hand still pointed in his general direction. He rotated back to make sure no more attackers had made it around the Magnificent Seven to attack from the rear. Every once in awhile a sniper would catch one of the wolves, and it would slow down enough for his men's rounds to tear it to pieces.

I won't be able to hear a damned thing for a week after this fight, he thought.

He scanned all around, eyes flitting to Sabine, who seemed preternaturally calm in this environment—he had no idea why. It was as if she had been shooting for decades. Hell, *centuries*. Her calm assurance with the pistols both he and James absolutely knew came from the strangers continued to baffle them.

Plus, her weapons killed the Weres, and quickly.

Then the young Asian woman yelled over her shoulder to Sabine, who nodded and smiled like a mischievous rat.

"Oh, holy shit!" Timothy called out. "I think I'm getting a bullet boner!"

—

Yuko had been released. Released from the inhibitions in her mind against killing due to balance, due to responsibility and role. Her early life had been about hacking, computers, logic, and puzzles—the destruction of inanimate objects.

Not wanton destruction like killing, blood and gore.

Akio had demanded she learn weapons and martial arts, and because of her physiology, she was better than any human alive could ever hope to be. But she lacked the one trait that would allow her to be one of the best in the world...

She lacked the *willingness* to kill for a long time.

She had been in fights, and she had defended and killed before through the years. But in these last few minutes she had taken more lives than in her previous one hundred and eighty years of living.

When she had told Akio she would be coming along and also fighting, she had made a decision—she was best as a follower. She handled the duties the Queen had placed on her over the years. But almost all of them had been forced on her, moving Yuko out of her comfort zone.

Yuko handled her roles well. But truth be told, she excelled as the right-hand person of a natural leader. Akio was not her leader; her leader was among the stars.

Now Michael was here, and Bethany Anne's command had been explicit: she was to do whatever it took to help him be safe.

Michael directed her focus and her guns towards the Weres that were attacking the humans.

Earlier, she had slipped into her armor, and it had felt sensuous. When she dropped the same pistols she had used for over fifteen decades into her holsters, her body had reacted in a way that surprised her.

She felt like a black widow, hungry for a coming orgasm of death. The feelings had left her confused, until Michael commanded them to attack.

Now? Now her face was alight in the ecstasy of joining the skills honed over the century and a half with the newfound liberty brought about by Michael's authority.

How could she up the amperage of the moment? She looked around and smiled.

"Sabine!" she called.

14

AKIO GLANCED AROUND AT THE REMAINING WOLVES, AND HIS EYES widened in shock.

"Focus!" Michael called, and Akio's sword sliced to his left, taking half the head off a wolf that assumed that because Akio wasn't looking directly at him, he would be caught unaware.

The Were's death was proof of that mistake.

Michael's point was spot on. He thought about it a moment, and realized this was the first time he had been taken by surprise on the battlefield in...

Hmmm, he couldn't remember. He smiled when he realized it was because of a woman the last time, as well.

Sabine backed up two steps and felt Yuko's back against her own. "Right!" Yuko yelled, and Sabine swung to her right, Yuko in perfect synchronization with her. The gentle contact was a new experience for Sabine, as the two danced in a circle and fired their weapons, continuing to move.

To dance.

To feel each other's power, keeping the entire battlefield in view as they turned together. Sabine didn't need to wonder if her legs could handle this. She had run for sport all her life, and she didn't just run over the flat streets in cities. No, she also ran through fields, over broken concrete, up mountains, and down ravines. Her feet never missed a step as they them rotated clockwise. If a wolf was far enough away, she left it for Yuko to take out as she focused on selecting targets and firing.

God, why hadn't she ever danced like this before?

That's when the pistol in her right hand clicked, empty.

"I've got you," a breath spoke in her ear as if on the wind. There was a tug on her belt and her right pistol was replaced by one of Yuko's. "Only fire that if you have to," Yuko said. Sabine nodded.

Fire left, left, left.

She felt for the new pistol with her right hand, then Yuko said, "Let's go left!"

Sabine swung to her left, knees slightly bent, as they continued their sensuous dance of death.

Michael glanced at the two women and smiled as he called to Akio, "Is Yuko acting out of character?"

"*Hai!*"

"She seems to be enjoying herself," he observed.

"That is true," Akio responded. "What did you do to her?"

"Me?" Michael asked as the dead and injured wolves continued to pile up. They had danced with their swords away from the line and were now some fifty yards away.

"Yes, Michael. This is not Yuko as I have known her." Akio mused. "So, I am making the supposition that you might have done something similar to the help I gave Sabine."

Michael laughed. "No, I think you are just constrained by your narrow minded focus and purpose, Akio. I suspect I know why she is channeling her inner Bethany Anne, but you would have to ask her to confirm my guess."

"No mental suggestions?" Akio queried as they continued

their fight against the wolves. Michael had taken one bite that he had almost healed from, and Akio had two bites and a slash across his chest that his armor had mostly deflected.

"Not my style with my own people, Akio," Michael replied. He was pleased to realize that Akio's questions hadn't angered him. Perhaps he was changing, at least a little. He decided he liked this new Michael.

"I'll have to ask, then," Akio agreed as he stabbed a Were that had gotten too close.

"You can resupply my pistols if I go empty, right?" Michael called back.

"*Hai!*"

There was a pause before Michael said to no one in particular, "I'm getting bored."

Akio, his eyes opening wide, turned to see what Michael was going to do as he protected his own left side.

"Oh shit!" Mark and Jacqueline both yelled at the same time.

"That's bad?" Eve questioned from their right, as two of the humans behind them asked what the problem was.

"Michael's bored," Mark called over his shoulder. Jacqueline stayed quiet. Speaking in this form annoyed her, and her blood lust was dropping.

Mark turned to his left, then his right. He was surprised to see his love had changed back to human again, and was reaching down for her staff. "Damn!" he swore, and swung his sword to keep a wolf a few steps back as Jacqueline grabbed her weapon and stood up. "Give a guy a little warning," he snapped at her.

Jacqueline purred her answer. "I knew you were *up* to the challenge, baby."

"Geez," Timothy said to James. "Another battle boner!"

"Catch!" Michael twisted to his left in a circle, tossed his sword towards Akio and dragged his coat back to reach his pistols. He unclipped the straps that held them in place and yanked.

As he finished his turn, Jean Dukes ready in both hands, Michael decided to see just how quickly he could react with the Etheric powering him.

Wolves started evaporating in a hail of small, powerful needles. The kinetic power bucked the pistols in Michael's hands as guts and entrails exploded into the air.

"That is just gross!" Jacqueline covered her head as the wind carried a mist of blood and guts down on top of them. Yuko and Sabine had stopped their circling dance and held their arms over their heads. The humans were looking around.

Except one. He was spitting gunk like he had gaped a little too long.

When he stopped, everyone slowly turned to look at the bald man who was covered in gore, a maniacal grin on his face.

"Why didn't anyone tell me to keep these on 11?" he asked.

Kirk, James and Timothy retired back to the planning warehouse after showing them where they could clean up. Yuko had informed everyone that they would have new clothes, or at least clean clothes, in an hour when she and Eve got back. For right now everyone had a robe, a towel, and some soap to go and take showers here in Kirk's headquarters.

What Akio didn't tell the rest was that Yuko would come back clean after using the advanced showers in their own base. Michael didn't want to leave, so no one else considered it.

He wondered what Jacqueline might say if and when she saw the facilities back in Japan? Right now the young woman was agitated from the gore, the stench and the stickiness from Michael's "I'm bored" episode. Mark had offered to help scrub her back in the shower and the next thing Akio knew, they had disappeared to get clean.

Michael came out of the showers in a robe, his holsters and pistols over his shoulder. He didn't require his sword, so that would go back into the container for now, but he wouldn't allow the pistols out of his sight.

"So." Kirk started the conversation. He, James and Timothy had chosen to talk before they cleaned up. Alan took the rest of the guys over to another building they'd claimed, to shower after the fight. "We have monsters on our side, too."

Timothy shrugged. "Yes," he agreed. "But they have really nice asses."

"Sabine isn't a monster," James said as he turned to nod in Timothy's direction. "And they do have nice asses."

"We *are* talking about the women, right?" Kirk asked, an eyebrow raised.

"Fuck it." Timothy smiled. "I don't usually judge my male counterparts, but the guys are all tight too."

Kirk and James laughed.

James exhaled as he looked at the other guys. "Let's face it, all of our people would be dead if not for them."

Kirk nodded. "You know that Sabine has been changed in some way? There's no way a normal human can shoot like that."

"She swears that the Akio guy," James replied, "taught her last night."

"C'mon," Kirk shook his head. "One lesson?"

"From a guy centuries old," Timothy interjected and Kirk eyed him. Timothy put up his hands. "Don't kill the messenger here, but time is a teacher for those who learn to teach in little time."

"Not to mention," James put in, "who knows what voodoo he can do?"

"He's a vampire," Kirk stated. "So is the other one, Michael."

"Well, Mark too," James added.

"Yes, but they're *our* vampires," Timothy exclaimed as the two shot him looks. "No, not like we own them, for fuck's sake. I mean they're on our team."

"Not sure we could call it our team so much as they stand between us and the others," James opined.

"That's probably it right there." Kirk pointed to James. "They're another faction, and they're here to fight the same shit we are. We aren't a team, so much as two teams fighting the same bad guys."

"Bad guys who were sending a shit-ton of Weres in our direction to kill us today," James agreed.

"Hey," Timothy broke in. "If it is all the same to you, I say we become the sub-team for the Magnificent Seven and help them help us. For the first fucking time in three years it feels like my future isn't just death by whatever nasty shit my brain can dream up."

"God help me," James turned to look at Kirk, "but I have to say I agree with him."

"What do you guys think the others will say?" Kirk asked them.

"That you are a fucking genius," Timothy said.

"What he said," James agreed, then grimaced. "Again."

Kirk raised his eyebrows and looked at James. "That's got to be some kind of record."

"That's because you both finally see the genius in my words," Timothy said smugly.

"That's the first time you've *had* any genius in your words," James shot back.

"Well," Timothy scratched his head, "okay, I grant you that." He smiled at his friends. "But I get to stand behind Yuko and Sabine again."

"Oh, *hell* no…" James started.

"Yeah," Kirk agreed, "no more battle boners for you."

Most of the humans who weren't manning the walls, such as

they were, watched as a large box slid silently down from the morning sky. It came to rest in the street just a half mile inside the city. Michael was waiting for Yuko and Eve as he stood in his robe just watching their container, painted solid black, slowly land.

The door opened slightly. "We have your clothes," Yuko called as Michael walked up, a door open wide enough for him to step inside. He nodded to both Yuko and Eve, who was standing quietly in a corner. Regardless of how curious those watching their craft were, no one cared to approach too closely.

The rumors, if anyone believed them, said the man was a day-walking vampire who could blow you up with his mind and cut your head off before you could blink.

And other unbelievable shit.

While the rumors might be wrong, they probably had a bit of truth to them, didn't they? Either way, no one chose to go knock on the door.

Yuko had Michael's clothes laid out inside. He dropped his robe to start changing, and Yuko averted her eyes.

He had a strong set of shoulders, that was for sure.

"Thank you, Yuko," Michael said, and she turned around again as he was sliding his coat back on. "It's amazing how you can get attached to something, and right now, this coat seems to help anchor me." He rubbed the left sleeve with his right hand. "Very clean." He looked up and smiled. "I imagine your shower was just as good?"

Yuko blushed. "There was a lot of blood in my hair."

"Sorry about that." Michael smiled mischievously. "Battle can be messy."

"Well, it can when you are at the forefront of it, yes," Yuko agreed. "I watched Akio while we fought. He seemed a little more…"

"Free?" Michael asked as she paused.

"Unrestrained." Yuko said. "I suppose you might say free. I think having you come back has affected us both."

"Akio said something about you acting differently as well. Not as concerned with killing as you were since Bethany Anne left?"

"My role was to be the diplomat after she left," Yuko told him, and Michael nodded for her to continue. "We were to sit tight, help where we could, and decide which trouble spots we should risk ourselves for when they weren't our primary mission." She looked up at Michael. "You are here, so now our primary mission is to protect you and neither of us are about to suggest you do anything but tell us how to help." She shrugged. "It has been liberating. I recognize that I work best when I am very assured of my path. When I was young, death and killing were foreign to me. I have learned over the decades to kill as needed. Now our path is to support you for when Bethany Anne comes back."

Michael narrowed his eyes. "There's no way back to her?"

"No, the gate was destroyed and we do not have a ship—" Yuko began but was interrupted by Eve.

"Not exactly," the little AI told the two.

Michael turned to look at Eve, and even Yuko looked at her friend with curiosity. "Go ahead," he said.

"We have been fighting the Wechselbalg in China for so many decades, so of course we know of many of the rumors," Eve said.

"Of course." Yuko nodded her head as her eyes went distant.

"What rumors?" Michael asked, searching his brain for any information. "I don't remember China having any type of space-craft. What happened after I was blasted into the Etheric?"

"Is that what happened?" Yuko asked, then her eyes widened and she clapped her hands twice in happiness. "Oh! Is that how Bethany Anne knew you were alive?"

Michael smiled at the excited woman. "Probably, although I don't think I was even remotely conscious for a long, long time. I wouldn't put it past her to have felt a connection when she traveled through the Etheric, though. She's much more sensitive to it than I am." He turned to Eve. "But I'd like to understand what you mean by the Chinese Wechselbalg?"

Eve answered. "Well, Bethany Anne fought a clan that came after us. We tracked down the last person, and she was part of a Wechselbalg pack that was working with a clan of Kurtherians."

Michael interrupted, "A different clan?"

"Yes," Eve responded.

"How the hell did so many different Kurtherians find our damned planet?" Michael mused.

Yuko just shrugged.

"Sorry, go on." Michael waved to Eve.

"We have solid information that the Wechselbalg in China have the components for a Kurtherian spaceship, but they can't put it together."

"Why would we be able to?" Michael asked.

"Because we know where there is another Kurtherian to ask, and we have Eve, of course," Yuko answered, nodding to the AI.

Michael thought about that for a moment, then another couple of moments, "ArchAngel?"

Yuko nodded in agreement as Michael asked, "What about Boris?"

Akio stepped into the container. "Still alive, with a wife and family." He walked over to the clothes that were next to Michael's and dropped his robe.

Yuko's eyes flashed to the ceiling in exasperation. "What is it with you guys not caring that there are two females present?"

"Why?" Michael asked, looking confused. "I was gone at least a hundred and fifty plus years. That would make you—"

Yuko's normally serene voice was a bit agitated. "Still able to feel embarrassed when guys drop their clothes around me, thank you, Michael."

Jacqueline came in as Akio finished buttoning his shirt. "Really, Yuko?" she asked the vampire as she padded over to her own clothes. "How about women?" she asked as she started to drop her robe.

"Oh for…" Yuko turned and walked out of the container as Michael and Jacqueline laughed behind her.

Akio looked at Michael, who winked back at him. "Trust me." This time, Michael smiled when Akio did a passable imitation of rolling his eyes.

Akio was trying, Michael had to give him that. Maybe Michael could help encourage this a little.

"Michael?" Yuko's voice came back to them. "You might want to come out here. We have new arrivals!"

15

MICHAEL CHECKED HIS PISTOLS AND HIS ULFBERHT SWORD AND walked out of the container to find the three main leaders of the humans.

They were still bloody.

"We were never properly introduced. I'm Kirk." The dark-haired man with a beard waved. "Sorry, too much blood to be shaking hands." He turned to point out his two compatriots. "The short blond one at the end is Timothy, and the gargantuan one next to me here is James."

"I'd just like to say," Timothy spoke next, "that I wasn't going to shoot you."

Michael raised an eyebrow before he started smiling. "Sorry, I just wanted to make sure you understood the consequences of aiming the rifle at me."

"The hell..." James breathed out.

Kirk looked over at him. "That's my line."

"Well," James replied, "you should use it more often." He turned to Michael. "You really did tell Timothy that you would shove the rifle up his ass?"

Yes, Michael answered. *Wouldn't you do something like that if someone was pointing a gun in your direction?*

"Well, of course." James said.

"Dude," Kirk hissed.

"One second, Kirk," James replied before looking back to Michael. "But how?"

Like, how did I contact him? Michael asked while his lips curved in a smile.

"Yeah," James asked.

Like this, Michael answered.

"Dude!" Kirk punched James.

James turned on his friend. "Son of a bitch, Kirk! The fuck?" he said as he rubbed his arm.

Kirk turned to point at Michael. "He's not talking!"

"The hell he isn't talking!" James replied. "We just had a—"

"Out loud," Kirk clarified.

"What?" James looked back at Michael.

Like I said. Michael told him. *Just like that.*

"Oh." James replied before turning to Timothy. "My apologies."

"I was right three times now?" Timothy confirmed.

James looked at his friend a moment. "I really fucking hate you."

"More attackers?" Michael tried to steer the conversation back to the relevant topic.

"Yeah, sorry." Kirk took back control. "We have scouts and ways to track the other two large Were populations, and they're on their way. Maybe two or three thousand more coming at us. They will arrive no later than a couple of hours from now."

"You have radio?"

"Limited, yes." Kirk agreed.

"Hmmm," Michael responded, as Akio walked up next to him.

"That might be fun, but it's too many to fight without spillage around us."

"Agreed," Michael answered. "Two pucks left?" Akio nodded to answer.

"How much time before they get here?" Michael asked Kirk for confirmation of the timeline.

"Two hours or so," Kirk said.

"Okay," Michael replied, and turned back to Akio. "Other weapons of mass destruction?"

Akio shrugged. "If we can make it back to base in time, we have some large bombs that would take out a small mountain."

"Impressive, but too much," Michael answered.

Mark joined the group as Jacqueline came out of the container. All three of the humans glanced at her before turning back to Michael.

Mark hugged her. "Your clothes are inside," she told him. "Make sure Yuko knows when you're ready to change, she's working on her blushing."

"I am not!" Yuko snapped as Sabine walked up.

"Mark is about to change," Yuko told her.

Sabine shrugged. "I don't care if he does," she replied and smiled. "I've seen his girlfriend and his eyes won't be wandering any time soon."

"Like ever," Jacqueline replied as she stared directly at Mark.

"Hey, I'm clean here. I just need clothes." He turned to Sabine. "You go first, I'll wait."

Sabine patted him on the shoulder as she walked past. "That's how you get the room to yourself, Yuko."

Yuko stared at the young woman, her head rotating to follow her as she continued into the container. She could hear Eve point out the clothes.

"Do we have a weatherman up there?" Michael asked, as he looked up at the clouds.

Akio pursed his lips and turned towards the container, but Eve's voice came out before he could ask. "Maybe a forty percent chance of rain when the Weres get here."

"Rain?" James and Timothy both asked.

"Not rain," Michael replied as his eyes searched the clouds. "Ammunition."

"Hey!" Sabine's voice came out of the container. "Who gets the kiss for the extra rounds?"

"That would be Yuko," Eve replied. Everyone turned to Yuko, whose cheeks were starting to turn red again.

"Um." Timothy interrupted. "Not to appear unappreciative for what you did this morning, but why does it seem you guys are not too worried about two thousand Weres?"

"Or more," James added.

"Or more," Timothy agreed, "coming our way right now?"

"You plan on fighting again?" Michael asked, and all of the men nodded. "Well, we'll be in a situation I happen to enjoy."

"What kind of situation is that?" Kirk finally asked when Michael said no more.

Michael smiled. "A target-rich environment." He looked at the buildings surrounding them. "Let's look at your defenses and figure out how to fortify them against the Wechselbalg."

"Sure." Kirk shrugged and turned to start walking back towards the front lines. "Have you fought these guys a lot, then?"

"Well," Michael said as Sabine came out and Mark replaced her. "I've killed a few in my time."

"Dude," Kirk's voice was fading as they walked away. "You killed hundreds this morning."

"Yes," Michael agreed. "But I was just warming up."

James and Timothy looked at each other, their eyes widening when Jacqueline snorted. They turned to her. "Is he kidding?" asked Timothy.

Jacqueline looked at Michael and Kirk as they walked away. "You know, I doubt it. If anything, he's probably underselling himself. He tends to be humble about his ability to turn live bodies into corpses."

Akio took a step towards Jacqueline. "What do you think he wants with the weather report?"

Jacqueline's face turned from thoughtful to slightly fearful. "He wants to fight the elements again, and turn them on those who would dare challenge him," she said softly as Mark walked up to the group.

"Who is challenging whom?"

"Michael," Jacqueline said as she leaned back against him. Mark's arms encircled her. "He's hoping the weather comes again."

"Oh, seriously?" Mark asked, and looked at the two distant figures. "That would be badass." Mark looked at the men watching him. "God bless, but if he starts raising his arms to the sky, drop everything and run like hell. It isn't a good place to be."

"Where isn't a good place to be?" James asked.

"With Michael," Jacqueline answered. "When he decides to fight with Mother Nature."

"You have some good defensive positions." Michael pointed to a few places below the two men who were standing at the top of a five-story building. There were open places and some wrecked buildings in front of them. The stench of the dead bodies was blowing to the southwest, thankfully. "But for this fight, I want you to pull your people back to this building," Michael then pointed to a similar one across the street, "and that one. Have your sharpshooters across the top and your fighters blocking the way up. Protect your shooters and harass the hell out of the Weres."

"That's going to leave us stuck up here," Kirk stated. "We'll be out of food and water with no way to resupply."

"We can get you off the top, but you won't need the help." Michael told him.

"Why?" Kirk asked. "I'm not doubting you, I'm just asking

because these people trust me and I need to know so that I can, in good conscience, tell them I recommend."

"Because the Weres might have numbers, but I have what matters."

Kirk asked. "What's that?"

Michael turned from looking out over the plain to look at Kirk. He eyes flashed red and his visage took on the expression that Kirk would later describe as 'a walking personification of Death.' His voice dropped an octave. "I have the assurance I will be meeting my love at the end of this. This is merely a small stopping point to take care of someone who should have stayed in the ground."

"The Duke?" Kirk asked.

Michael nodded. "His name, if I were to make an educated guess, is William Renaud. I thought he was dead after this amount of time. I'm not sure what idiots raided that crypt, but they would certainly have paid for their mistake."

Kirk thought about his comment. "What assurance?"

Michael smiled. "Why, Kirk, I gave her a promise to come back and I'll keep it, no matter how many stand between me and that day."

"So why not just find the Duke and kill him?" he asked. "Why get involved in this?"

"That," Michael replied, "would be dishonorable, Kirk." Michael's eyes flashed red again as they narrowed, and he looked at the horizon. "One thing I'm not, is dishonorable."

The humans who had chosen to stay in Paris for the fight were holed up in the two buildings Michael had designated. Kirk and his people were on top of the building where Michael had spoken to Kirk. "They want us up here why?" Timothy asked.

"Trust me," Kirk replied. "He never said why, just *do it*." He turned from watching the Magnificent Seven walking down the street between the two buildings and out onto the plain. "If I had to guess, they're going to pull some serious shit and don't want us in the way."

"Or hurt," James added.

Kirk turned to James and thought about his comment. "Yeah, actually you're probably right."

"You know," Mark said as they walked about a quarter mile from the buildings, "you could always make sure it rains."

"Hmmm?" Michael asked and turned to Mark. "What do you mean?"

"Well, what about doing the opposite of what you did in the clouds?" Mark asked. "Seems like it might work."

"Maybe, but I was actually up in the clouds at the time." Michael replied. "We're on the ground."

"So what happens if we get no lightning?" Jacqueline asked. "I mean, I'm not chickening out, but I have a date tonight and frankly, getting gory really isn't my cup of tea. And two thousand?"

"It won't be two thousand," Akio said as he pulled out a tablet.

"Oh shit!" Mark exclaimed. "Dude, you have a tablet?"

Jacqueline slapped his arm. "Hey, Technolust Boy, pay attention over here."

"Always, baby," Mark threw her a kiss. "But c'mon!"

Jacqueline nodded. "Okay." As Mark let go of her hand and walked over next to Akio as she huffed, "Nerds."

"No," Michael replied. "The correct term is *geek*."

"What's the difference?" Jacqueline asked.

"Um…" Michael thought about that a moment. "Nerds are more into science for science's sake. Geeks are more into general smart stuff, not just science, and they love all things computer." He paused a moment. "I'll have to ask Tabitha about that some time to make sure I have it right."

"Oh no you don't!" She pointed at Mark, who was paying attention to them. "I saw you raise your head when she-who-shall-not-be-named was spoken of!" Mark dropped his head and continued his conversation with Akio.

"Jacqueline," Michael said, "you need to realize that you have a wonderful guy in Mark, so don't run him off with jealousy."

"Yeah, I know," she answered, "but he doesn't give off the same scent as a mated Were, and it's driving my inner wolf fucking crazy."

"You're both human," Michael chided her, "not another version of Romeo and Juliet." Michael pursed his lips. "I guess that isn't exactly the right metaphor, actually."

"Who?" she asked.

Michael just shook his head in exasperation. "A story for the ages. And apparently, another victim of the last war."

Jacqueline giggled. "I'm just kidding Michael. I know who they are."

Michael eyed the young woman, then shook his head and smiled.

Then all seven of them turned as one to the north.

Sabine looked in that direction. "What the hell, people? Aren't they coming from the west?"

"Yes," Eve agreed, "but that thunder we just heard was coming from the north."

Gerard set up his lunch table, then pulled a red and white checkered tablecloth from the bag and laid it out. He noticed the storm coming. It should wash away some of the yuckiness from the killing that was going to happen soon. He laid his bread and cheese, and the bottle of wine he had been saving for a special occasion.

He hoped it hadn't spoiled.

The rest were on the bottom floor of this tenement. He had seen the rooftop when they had arrived in Paris, and marked it as a good place for a picnic. Since Paris had some light, but not in all places, it might do for a nighttime destination on the night of a full moon.

Not tonight, though. He had plans and meetings before the Duke woke up. Gerard figured he would take the two Alphas and their seconds with him for a meeting with the Duke and his six lieutenants.

Akio turned the tablet so that Mark could see it. "We are watching the satellites above us. We have some ability to see through the thickening cloud cover, but it is starting to degrade fast. However, such a large mass of hot bodies will show up here." Akio touched a button on the screen.

"That is so cool!" Mark replied. "What are we going to do?"

Akio punched the first button. "Did you know that often it isn't the size of the projectile but rather how much kinetic energy it carries that determines the amount of damage it can do?

"No," Mark replied. "I know the math. Well, sort of," he clarified. "But how something really small can create a massive amount of damage is beyond me."

Akio looked around like he was searching out a spy before he looked at Mark and whispered, "Me too!" and gave the young man a wink.

Half a second later, Eve called out, "I heard that!"

Akio turned towards Eve and smiled. For an AI, she did a remarkable approximation of a double take. She went back through her memory banks and couldn't locate one other instance where she had personally witnessed him smiling. His nanocytes must have been working extra hard to fix those unused muscles.

Lilliana was one of the few female Alpha Weres anywhere in Europe, at least as far as she knew. She had grown up with three brothers who didn't care what bodily attributes she had. It was a free-for-all, and she was the second oldest.

Her brother Marcel at the top had tried to push his authority down, and her brothers Terrence and Edward had tried to fight and claw their way up the sibling chain of rivalry. She wasn't a beauty; she was built like an ox. She had muscles, and walked with a rolling forward momentum in her human form.

Two of her brothers had been gone for fifteen years now. The youngest, Edward, was the only one who had left, he had gone east to look for his future. The other two had stayed and challenged the previous Alpha, Clement. Clement had torn Terrence apart rather easily, and she had shaken her head at that. For three months, she had argued with that blockhead that he wasn't strong enough to take Clement. So she had tried to teach him, to work with him, and finally she had almost killed him herself to prove he wasn't ready.

All it did was make him more determined to challenge for the Alpha position. Lilliana had hung her head and kissed him goodbye. She wouldn't watch the killing. If she could take him out, then so could many others in the pack. Either way, Terrence wasn't going to be alive for long.

Within two weeks of Terrence failing to prevail, Marcel came to her. Enough ridicule had been thrown Marcel's way about Terrence that he had decided he must challenge.

This time, she and Marcel practiced for six months in secret. In the end, Lilliana had beaten Marcel most of the time, but she had to agree that without her superior strength and knowledge of him, having fought since they were both young, she might not have been so successful.

He encouraged her to come and witness the fight. When Marcel raised his neck in surrender to Clement, both wolves were torn and bloody, and Lilliana felt proud of the display Marcel had managed. There was respect for him, and she could tell that the pack expected him to become the Second, behind Clement.

Until Clement snapped Marcel's exposed throat.

"I challenge!" Lilliana had demanded before the light in her brother's eyes had even faded.

Clement, smug in his ability, merely changed back to human form. He kicked her dead brother to the side and told her, "Give me fifteen minutes."

Lilliana nodded, her face grim.

Fifteen minutes later, Clement changed and the fight was on.

16

THE STORM WASN'T LARGE FOR THIS TIME OF THE YEAR, BUT IT WAS active. As the weather moved across the countryside, the hot moist air from the ground rose into the cool atmosphere, and the clouds turned darker.

Lilliana remembered the fight with Clement. Only a few minutes into the challenge she had ripped a chunk out of his left hind leg.

There was no mercy in her eyes when he realized his mistake: he had taken down two of her family, and he thought she was the weak one.

He never realized she was the strongest.

She cared about her family, and for this asshole to have taken them out so cavalierly was not acceptable. She never let him have enough time to get his wind back. When someone gave his throat to the leader in submission, the leader shouldn't kill him.

Which is why she hated what she was doing now and running toward Paris.

The Duke had made it abundantly clear he was willing to kill indiscriminately until he was accorded the acceptance he required. She would give up her own life, but she wouldn't give up the lives of her pack. It was either do this with the Saberhall Pack, or the Duke was going to start gutting children tonight and they would never be free from him.

May God have mercy on her soul for what she was about to lead her pack into.

Michael could feel the vibrations in the ground and through the air. They were as discordant as the sound made by a bow being pulled across the strings of an out of tune violin.

"Wait right here," he told them, then disappeared.

"The hell?" Kirk asked, binoculars to his face. "Did Michael just disappear?"

Timothy, scope affixed to his rifle again, aimed where Kirk was looking for just the shortest amount of time, then agreed, "Yup."

James had nothing to say at all.

"Where do you think he went?" Kirk asked.

"If I had to guess," Timothy answered, scope a few inches from his eye as he adjusted it and looked around the space below, "I'd have to say I don't have one fucking clue."

"He went to go check on those werewolves," James said.

The two guys turned to look at him. "Seriously?" Kirk asked. When James nodded and touched his head, Kirk mouthed, "The hell…"

James popped Kirk on the chest and laughed. "No! I'm bull-shitting you." Kirk flipped his friend off and turned back around. "Asshole."

"But," James continued, "it makes sense. Where else does he have to go? You both should know he isn't going to leave his friends down there. Do any of them seem bothered?"

"Only the young American girl. She seems all sorts of annoyed."

Kirk turned his binoculars towards Jacqueline, who was walking in a circle looking generally displeased. He tried to read her lips and relayed to the others, "I... can't... believe... something something... that... asshole... left me... something else... Prick."

Timothy snickered. "She's not happy to be left behind."

"Damn!" James shrugged. "Pretty or not, she's too much work. Good thing that guy is a vampire. Putting up with her mouth all the time would be a pain in the ass."

"Are you going to tell her?" Kirk asked.

"Hell no," James replied. "You going to tell her you think she has a nice rack?"

"Hell no."

Rayane enjoyed the feel of the fertile soil as his clawed feet scraped the ground. He continued his run towards the city.

When he had commanded his pack to follow most had agreed, showing the same amount of bloodlust in their eyes as he had in his own. He had known that useless excuse for an Alpha, Adorjan, wouldn't be able to pull off killing the humans.

Rayane didn't believe the humans could hold out against all of the Weres, but he should have figured that Adorjan's pack wouldn't have been able to take them. Now it would just be his pack and Lilliana's, and while she could keep her own pack in line, they were a bunch of live-and-let-live believers in supporting everyone, no matter how superior someone was.

To hell with that.

His pack was now almost twelve hundred strong since he had taken in the survivors of two other packs, their Alphas dead due to mouthing off around the Duke.

Rayane didn't care any more for the Duke than did any other Wechselbalg, but he wasn't stupid either. His hot head and loud mouth were muzzled any time any vampire was around. That way his own pack was increased by over five hundred members without having to fight.

He had considered challenging Lilliana, but first he would need to finish getting rid of the troublemakers in his own pack. That's why he personally chose those hotheads to be in the front with him. At the very end he would slow down, howl his command to strike, and let those idiots be cannon fodder. His mission would be accomplished. Then, he would continue the attack, and dinner would be served.

Well, not dinner exactly, he wasn't one of those who ate humans.

Rayane missed a step when his mind wandered for just a moment, recent events flashing through his mind. A second later his mind cleared, and he streaked towards the city.

Lilliana, running ahead of her pack, wasn't pushing as hard as she could, and with good reason. What was she rushing towards?

Better for that jerk Rayane and his bloodthirsty crew to get there first, it would save her people some of the atrocities they would have to perform.

As long as she got to the city, the Duke wouldn't treat them ill, even if he chose to punish her for failing to join the attack at the same time as the other pack.

Whatever happened, she wouldn't lead her pack like that useless Clement had.

Though her mind wandered a moment thinking about her past, her feet knew where to step and her pack continued their advance.

Jacqueline kept pacing. "I'm telling you, he could have at least told us where he was going!" She threw her right arm into the air. "Is it too much to ask, really?"

"Yes," Michael replied.

Jacqueline stopped and turned around.

Akio noticed that she was both annoyed and relieved. *She is bitching because you scared her.*

Life is scary, and I don't need a mother, Michael responded

"Would it be too much to ask that you let us know what's going on?" she got out. "We're out here in the middle of a goddamned grass plain next to the city of never-being-lit anymore, and you up and disappear!" She walked up to him, then slowly and gently pounded on his chest. She looked up into his eyes and said softly, "You are the only connection I have to my father, Michael. You're the only one I can come to and ask questions."

Michael's annoyance softened. He reached out, and Jacqueline leaned into his arms. "I'm sorry, Jacqueline, I didn't think about how it would be for you. You're always such a strong woman, and I am very accustomed to doing whatever I like, because who's going to tell me I can't?"

From Michael's chest, a muffled voice answered, "Bethany Anne?"

Michael grinned. "She isn't here at the moment, so I can only get in trouble one time for everything I do before she gets back."

"No, that's not true." Jacqueline replied with a slight laugh. "I can save up all the little things and then tell her over many months. Each time I'll tell a worse story than the one before."

"She isn't going to buy that kind of shit."

Jacqueline pulled away, and wiped a tear from her eyes. "Why not?"

"She doesn't believe in drawing out emotional angst. Say it, get it done and move on would be her motto. She would see right through your attempt to get me in trouble, and teach you how inappropriate it is."

"And that," Akio interjected, "would not be a wise path, young one."

Jacqueline turned to Akio. "Why not?"

Yuko answered, causing Jacqueline to swivel her gaze again.

MICHAEL ANDERLE

"Because Bethany Anne holds her remedial classes on the sparring mat."

"She believes that the best lesson," Eve finished, causing Jacqueline complete her rotation, "is one where pain drives the learning process."

"Ooohhh." Jacqueline finally understood and turned back to Michael. "How about you promise to remember that inside this grown-up woman is still a young girl?"

Michael pulled her close one more time. "That's true for every woman, Jacqueline." He looked to the west, where he could sense the first pack getting closer.

"Even Bethany Anne."

Kirk lowered the binoculars. "If I hadn't seen it with my own two eyes," he handed the binoculars to James, "I would never have believed that a vampire could have a family."

"Why?" James asked as he dialed in on the group in front of them. "What's… Oh. Was she crying?"

"Yup," Timothy answered. "The whole group was telling her something. I think she was just scared that Michael left."

"She knows how badass the others are, right?" James asked.

"Dude, maybe he's like her dad or something. It doesn't matter what happens if your dad disappears and you aren't expecting it. Kiss everything else goodbye."

"Fuck." Kirk laughed. "If that's her father figure, imagine the size of the pair Mark must have to have asked her on a date."

Timothy chimed in, "Yeah, I've got to give him credit. That guy could be in for a world of hurt. He's taking one for the team, there."

"Yeah, but nobody is going to mess with him or his girl."

Everyone on top of the building looked out at the horizon, where a huge number of wolves were starting to bear down on them.

Kirk said, "I hope the Magnificent Seven are up to this."

A rifle cocked behind Kirk. "Let's get our own as well," a voice added behind the trio.

"Akio?" Michael said.

"*Hai.*"

"What say we use both pucks this time?"

"*Hai,*" Akio agreed and looked over at Eve. She nodded and moments later, the ground rumbled as dirt and wolves flew into the air. Yips, growls, howls, and keens of pain could be heard as hundreds of bodies sailed through the air to scatter among the shrubs and trees.

"Those with pistols!" Michael pulled his coat back, exposing his twin pair of Jean Dukes. "It's time we truly use our Kurtherian enhancements." Michael looked towards the coming storm, a smile on his face. "Don't hold back."

"I'm getting some damned pistols or something next time," Jacqueline muttered as Mark rubbed her back.

"*Fire.*"

Rayane felt the second explosion before the first registered in his brain. He turned his head, and his eyes widened in shock as he saw many of his pack flying through the air. Pieces of wolves raining down around him told him that he had lost countless pack members already.

So this was how Adorjan had failed. It wasn't because they were as pitiful as he suspected, but rather that the humans had weapons the Duke didn't know about.

Rayane's eyes narrowed. *Or didn't share.*

It would be just like that self-absorbed prick not to tell them about weapons that could hurt his pack. He would expect them to succeed regardless of the cost. It didn't matter that it wasn't the pack's way of doing things.

But it was a vampire's.

Rayane briefly considered turning his pack around, then

reality hit. He knew if he did that he wouldn't last a month before the Duke came calling. He turned back towards the city and howled, ordering his pack forward.

Lilliana heard the explosions to the north. She glanced over and saw the thunderstorm, but what she had felt didn't seem like thunder. Rather, it was as if the Earth itself had trembled.

It certainly didn't feel right. She howled a command and they slowed down just a little bit more.

"That," Akio agreed as the wolves came into view, "is a very target-rich environment."

Michael had been the only one firing so far. When he began shooting, he'd been taking out a wolf at the rate of one every two seconds. Now he was up to approximately one wolf per second. Then Akio started firing. A couple of moments later, Yuko's pistol joined in.

They had about a minute before the line hit them.

Eve walked a little way forward and turned so that her left shoulder was slightly forward. She raised her leg and slammed it into the ground. She looked behind her. "Shame, no Alan this time."

Mark walked over and started making a hole for his own foot. "I got your back, Eve. This time, you aren't flying anywhere."

"Big words for a..." Eve looked Mark up and down, "big vampire. You are bigger up close."

"Yes, he's bigger than he looks." Jacqueline winked at the AI as she got behind Mark and braced his back. "Let's rip them up, Eve."

Eve turned around and activated her guidance system. She watched wolves dropping from the massed fire that Michael, Akio, and Yuko were bombarding them with. She wondered when Sabine would join in.

"Remember, this kicks hard!" she told them as she unholstered her micro rocket gun and aimed it at the approaching horde. No one so far was targeting the Weres off to the right, so she put her reticules on them—a total of twenty-five—and counted down. "Three, two, one, pull!" She locked her arm and squeezed the trigger. The twenty-five little missiles kicked like a mule, but this time Mark had relocated his arms quickly enough that not only didn't she fly backwards, she didn't fall to the ground either. At the very end, she could feel him letting her fall backward into his open arms and chest.

"Owww, cracked rib!" He coughed as Eve stepped out of his protective hold. They watched twenty-five... no, twenty-four Weres explode, peripherally causing a few additional Weres to fall over. "Dog pile!" Mark laughed as they noticed two or three places where the Weres tripped and fell over each other.

They turned as they heard Sabine's guns kick in.

"Now," Michael said, "we make them pay!"

ALMIGHTY GOD! RAYANE LOOKED AROUND AS WERE AFTER WERE died. *Who the hell were these seven people in front of them?*

And why was he feeling so hot?

"Michael!" Jacqueline called out. "There's still a shitload of Weres on the way!"

They had to be killing between fifteen and twenty Weres a second, but the Weres kept coming.

"They are a bit hard-headed," Michael agreed. "This pack isn't worth saving, so I'm not going to try."

"There's another pack that *is* worth saving?" Akio asked.

Mark piped up, "You'd try saving them?"

"Yes. The second pack will be arriving perhaps ten minutes after the first," Michael said, his rhythmic shooting continuing faster and faster. "Dammit! I missed."

"You did?" Akio asked. "I didn't see a miss."

"That's because I aim low so if I miss my target, I still get a chance at one behind them." In a flash, Michael swung his hands down and holstered his pistols. "It's time to take this old-school."

"You're going to use a sword on them?" Sabine asked, her pistols firing methodically left, right, left, right.

"Who said anything about a sword?" Michael responded, smiling. "I'm talking about bringing a little mad and angry back into the equation."

First, their Alpha went up in flames, his yelp of pain sharp before he died. Then, the man in the front started walking towards the pack.

Those in front yipped in fear when his eyes flared red.

"Uh oh…" Kirk mumbled, his eyes glued to the binoculars.

"What?" Timothy asked. He had given his gun to James, who had taken a few shots at the Weres. The shots were more annoying than damaging, as the team didn't have nearly enough silver ammunition.

"Michael's moving," James answered Timothy.

"Where?" he asked.

"Walking towards the Weres." Kirk lowered the binoculars and turned to James. "Does it look like he walks super-fast? Does he walk as fast as most people run?"

"No fucking clue," James replied over the constant firing from their rooftop and the many windows below, as the team continued shooting at the Weres.

"You guys need to step back a bit," Michael called over his shoulder. "I don't need you to get randomly electrocuted."

"Ooohhhh, shit." Jacqueline grabbed Eve's shoulder. "C'mon little lady, it isn't a good idea to be close."

"Why?" she asked.

"Because," Mark answered, "it's about to get scary as hell down here."

Akio heard Mark's answer and told Yuko to back up. He grabbed Sabine, who was still shooting, and carried her away. Michael's hands were slowly starting to glow a bluish-white.

\---

The thunder hurt Lilliana's ears, and the sudden lightning near the city surprised her. It was too much—too fast and too consistent to be natural.

And if it wasn't natural, then who was pulling lightning from the sky?

Lilliana howled another command, and the pack slowed to a simple jog.

The Duke could kiss her furry ass. She wasn't running into an unnatural storm.

\---

A woman's voice came from the rooftop. "Oh. My. God!"

Kirk looked to his right to see Greta standing next to him. She was a short woman with sandy brown hair and freckles. Her blue eyes pierced the dark afternoon sky as the lightning flashed down to a central location in front of them.

The bolts of fire reflected from those blue orbs. The sharp light cast shadows all around them, the thunder deafening.

The power humbling.

The screams of those who had changed from wolf form back to human. A keening in the dark of the day. The cries for mercy, for compassion, for help. All ignored by the man in the coat.

"Michael the ArchAngel," Kirk whispered. "No one should ignore the power he wields, since God sent him to Earth."

"He," Greta assured him, "is no angel."

\---

"Shit, fucking shit!" Jacqueline said as Mark grabbed her and Eve in an embrace, their hair standing up in the ionized air. "My damned ears are bleeding!"

Mark sniffed. "No, they aren't!"

Eve made a noise. "She's trying to make a point." Eve turned to look up at him. "You need some help understanding women!"

Mark snorted. "I'm going to need a *lot* of help to understand women," he agreed. "But she knew I was a geek when she met me."

"And he was so skinny!" Jacqueline added over the booming of the thunder.

"He really gets his mad on, doesn't he?" Sabine asked from the shelter of Akio's arms around her and Yuko.

"Now I see why Bethany Anne likes him so much," Yuko agreed.

"Whhhhaaatttt?" Sabine asked. "What kind of crazy lady wants a man that throws lightning around?"

Akio chuckled. "One that throws fireballs."

There was a pause as the thunder rolled over them.

Sabine responded with a quiet, "Oh."

This time Michael was a bit better at pulling the ionized energy out of the clouds and redirecting it into the Wechselbalg. His first bolts were haphazard, only vaguely aimed towards the group of wolves coming at them.

That's when he figured out he could simply direct Etheric energy in streams towards his targets, and the lightning would follow the paths.

Now he was killing by the score. Most of the Wechselbalg had stopped trying to make it to the city as more and more, both wolf and human, died. Multiple wolves had changed, screaming in fear, hands over their ears as they rolled on the ground in anguish.

Their pleas for mercy went unanswered.

"Well, fuck." Kirk looked around, noticing that the darkness of the clouds was lifting.

"What, fuck?" Greta asked, comforted by Kirk's arm on her

shoulder. She looked up, following his eyes. "The storm is tapering off?"

"Yeah, I think so," Kirk agreed. He looked down at the group below. "Not that many left, but Wechselbalg are a hardy bunch."

James heard them talking. "That's the Magnificent Seven down there. Don't count them out just yet!"

"Guns forward!" Kirk yelled. "It's time we helped a little!"

\-\-\-

The two hundred semi-healthy Wechselbalg who still had their wits about them all heard the same speech in their ears.

My name is Michael... I am the first, and if any of you continue to fight me and my friends, I will be the last vampire you ever see. I am the darkness. I am the ArchAngel. Continue on pain of death.

\-\-\-

Lilliana slowed her jog then stopped and howled her orders to the pack. She changed back to her human form and looked at her second. "Guy, take the pack back three miles." She looked toward the city. "I have been commanded to go forward."

Guy transformed to human himself. His strong frame was imposing to most, but he had no desire for the top spot. "The Duke is not going to treat you well, Lilliana. At least let the pack support you."

Lilliana had been looking at the city, but she tilted her head towards Guy. "I am not being called by the Duke, but rather by someone from myth and legend." She started walking towards the city. "I'm being called by the Patriarch, Guy!"

Her second's face scrunched in confusion for a few moments, trying to remember where he had heard that name before. "Oh, blessed Mother of Christ!" He made the sign of the cross over his chest before turning to the pack. "We follow our Alpha's command!" He changed back into a wolf and started running around the throng to take the lead in the retreat.

THE CATACOMBS UNDER PARIS

THE CONSTANT POUNDING of the earth above him caused small but consistent shockwaves, and William Renaud woke up. His internal clock told him the sun was still up, but the destruction above was pleasing to him.

He slowly closed his eyes, a smile gracing his lips.

OUTSIDE PARIS

THE OCCASIONAL PISTOL shot barked as light rains caressed the living and the dead. Michael allowed the pack, at least those who only sought to grab their friends or the wounded, to carry them from the battlefield. Five times, Michael asked a Wechselbalg a question, and twice Michael pulled his sword from its sheath, beheaded the Were and had his blade back in its sheath before the body dropped to the ground.

Michael? Akio sent.

Hmmmm?

I see a lone Wechselbalg female approaching from the south.

Yes, that would be Lilliana. Allow her to approach; she will not be a problem. Have Jacqueline go and greet her.

I understand.

A moment later, Jacqueline started jogging in the direction of the lone, naked woman. She called over her shoulder, "We have any extra clothes?"

"I got 'em,'" Mark called back.

"Don't worry," Eve stopped him. "They will be delivered."

Mark looked over towards the city, seeing the container coming across the rooftops and heading towards the lone woman.

Lilliana smelled the death before she saw it. When she saw it, she was frightened by the utter devastation of Adorjan's pack. She noticed a few dead among the corpses littering the ground who were from Rayane's pack; that scared her to her core.

When the Duke wanted to hurt the pack, he killed the leaders or a few of the children. Even he wouldn't be able to kill so many so quickly.

This was a killing field. Who would be able to stop those that killed so many?

Lilliana stopped when she saw the young woman in a body-hugging black suit trotting towards her. She watched her for a moment before something else caught her eye, and she turned to look towards the city.

There was a box floating in the air, heading towards them. She considered fleeing, but doubted she would be able to outrun something that flew.

"You are from him?" Lilliana asked as Jacqueline came closer. "And that?" She nodded towards the container coming down just twenty paces away from them.

"That," Jacqueline answered as she turned to head to the container, "was sent to provide you with clothes, I imagine. One second." Jacqueline turned the locks and pulled on the handle. Nothing happened.

"Password, Please."

"Dammit, Eve!"

"Permission to enter approved," a mechanical voice answered.

"Who knew an AI had a sense of humor?" Jacqueline groused, and turned the handle to open the door. The lights turned on inside, and she walked in. She pulled on a drawer handle.

Nothing.

"Damn," she muttered. She found the switch that unlocked them all, and opened drawers until she found a suit similar to her own. By then the naked woman was peeking inside the container.

"Do I come in?" Lilliana asked as she stuck her head in. She whistled in appreciation of the weapons on display. "What I couldn't do with a few of these!"

"You wouldn't have time to find out," Jacqueline answered.

"Oh, I think I would," Lilliana pushed back, asserting her Alpha status to intimidate the young woman. She might be here under duress, but she could smell the Wechselbalg on this girl, and there was no way she was taking any lip from her.

"Accept the clothes, and don't make me bitch-slap you into next week," Jacqueline replied, her eyes dancing with yellow fire. "Michael will not be pleased to have to wait on your tardy ass."

Lilliana's hackles went up. "That is no way to speak to your betters," she snarled. Vampires were one thing, you didn't fuck with them. But Wechselbalg were another. She hadn't taken any shit from Clement, may evil eat his soul, or Adorjan or Rayane. She wasn't taking any from this young wannabe.

"What do you think is happening?" Yuko asked Akio and Michael, who were discussing the fight. Mark, Eve and Sabine drifted closer, looking at the distant container.

"I can tell you," Eve said to them.

Michael didn't look. "They're playing a game of Who's the Biggest Bitch."

"Hey now," Mark exclaimed, then started wondering what he was going to say if Michael asked him to follow up his comment.

He didn't.

"Bitch, female dog, Werewolf. It's a common term, Mark." Michael replied as he looked at the container just in time to hear the first howl from a wolf.

Followed a fast moment later by a howl from a monster. The next thing they saw was a large wolf being tossed out of the container to land about thirty feet away, rolling on the ground before she came to a stop. A huge female Pricolici followed her, mad as hell and not willing to take any more shit from anyone.

"I amm soo fucking tirredd of taaking shiiit from everyyyone who mmouuths offf too mmeeee!" Jacqueline growled as she walked towards the female wolf, who was getting up and making her own noises of annoyance.

Lilliana dove forward, not waiting for a repeat of her surprise from the first time. When the young woman had changed to a Pricolici, she had hesitated long enough for the girl to grab her and throw her out. She aimed for the calf, trying to mess up her legs.

That's when the world went upside down. The ribs on her right side felt crushed, and her snout was full of grass. She was starting to heal, her bones mending, when a clawed hand grabbed her and lifted her into the air face up. "You can gooo naakeed." By the time she was ready to make another try at the girl, she was close enough to see everyone watching them.

She was also close enough to realize that three of those standing there were day-walking vampires. She could curse her stupidity. She had allowed her frustrations to get the best of her, and now what position was she in?

She was fucked, that was for sure. She had just smelled that young male vampire and she recognized the same scent was on this woman.

She had attacked and tried to make some damned vampire's girlfriend submit.

She truly had her head up her own ass.

18

MICHAEL NODDED TO YUKO. SHE TURNED AND WALKED PAST Jacqueline and the new arrival, who was being carried like a pup. Jacqueline didn't even seem to be straining to hold up the large wolf. Eve had brought the container closer, so Yuko headed in and found the clothes that Jacqueline had pulled out before they had their disagreement.

She grabbed the clothes and took them back outside. The female Wechselbalg was on the ground, it looked like Jacqueline had just dropped her. She had changed at Michael's command.

Yuko walked over. "Here," she said to catch the woman's attention. "Wear this."

Lilliana nodded to the new lady, a vampire as well, then stood up and pulled on the one-piece suit. The fabric wasn't what she expected. It stretched wonderfully, and now she looked like she was a member of this group.

"No, you are not." Michael told her. When she looked at him, he continued. "This group has forged relationships. You just attacked one of us who was trying to give you clothing. No matter the rationalization, that was not acceptable."

Lilliana stayed quiet. All the death around her was distressing enough. She didn't need to add one more body to the count.

"You are the Alpha of the other pack of Weres the Duke sent to attack Paris," Michael said. "I permitted your pack to live because I looked at your history as you led them here." Lilliana's eyes grew round.

"Don't be surprised. I know more." Michael assured her. "The important thing you need to decide is whether you intend to take advantage of this opportunity, or shall I have Jacqueline kill you now and take over the pack?"

"Oh, *hell* no!" Jacqueline looked at Michael in disgust. She no more wanted to run a pack than she wanted kids at the moment. Either one of them was a lot of work, sacrificing yourself for a bunch of snot-nosed malcontents. He winked at her as Lilliana answered quickly.

"No!" she got out, before Jacqueline had finished speaking. She turned to see Jacqueline's expression of concern mirror her own. She no more wanted to give up her pack than this woman wanted to run it. She could tell that the young woman could easily have beaten her in a challenge, but running a pack wasn't in her future.

At least for now.

Lilliana hung her head. "I apologize. I acted inappropriately. It was a good reminder that there is always someone who can surpass you."

Jacqueline wanted to hate this Alpha, but her humility around Michael made it hard. Then again, if someone wasn't humble around Michael, he usually took care of it.

A small smile graced her face as she thought of Mark. Michael took very little shit from anyone, except Mark and herself.

—

"So, there are the Duke, his six followers and this one human named Gerard?" Michael asked, looking for confirmation from Lilliana.

"Yes." she agreed. "Rumor is that the Duke will come out at midnight tonight to accept the city from Gerard. He was the one who sent the message to attack the city."

"When?" Michael asked.

"When what? When did he tell us?"

Michael nodded.

"He sent the command earlier this morning."

"So," Michael turned around and looked out over the city, "he could be somewhere nearby, then."

"Or," Akio interrupted, "he has air capability and has seen us from a distance. Perhaps the people in the last pack signaled before they died? Some prearranged meeting or contact they failed to attend?"

"True, there is more than one possibility," Michael made a face. "Although I'm going to go see if I can find him. I would like to meet this…" he turned to Lilliana, an eyebrow raised.

"What?"

"What is he?" Michael asked.

"Human," she answered.

"No!" Jacqueline denied, eyes wide.

INSIDE PARIS

THE BUILDING WAS the highest that Gerard could find that he trusted not to collapse on him. He had used his device three times now, and no one had responded. Either the packs were still attacking—unlikely, since he heard nothing like battle sounds coming from the west—or they were dead, or had decided to betray the Duke.

If they were dead, he would need better information for the Duke when he woke up. If they had decided to betray the Duke, then he needed data so that he could best advise the Duke.

It moved towards late afternoon as he considered his options.

Two minutes later, he exited the building and headed towards the entrance to the catacombs. There was a time and a place for everything, but being found by a bunch of humans who would be worried about their safety after these attacks wasn't one of them.

OUTSIDE PARIS

JACQUELINE MOVED OVER TO MICHAEL, who had one eyebrow raised. He hadn't reacted as far as she could tell, but her outburst wasn't appreciated.

At all.

"I'm sorry." She put on the same face she had used for her dad when her emotions ran ahead of her mouth.

He nodded his acceptance, and she saw that the hard edges of his eyes had softened. It was the only tell her subconscious picked up about his feelings. No wonder a lot of older women went after younger men, they were so much easier to understand, and probably much easier to deal with. Bethany Anne was seriously taking one for the team when she chose to connect with Michael, that was for sure.

"I don't want you going out alone. You don't know what this guy has cooked up, if he's even here, and I don't want to wait if you don't come back for how long… another hundred and fifty years?"

Michael's lips pressed together as he reached up to fix his hair. When his hand touched his bald scalp, his eyes once again flashed with annoyance.

She never got tired of him being pissed about his missing hair.

"Akio and I will go," he told her, putting a hand on her shoulder and nodding to Mark. "You and Mark need to go with Yuko and Eve back to Japan."

"What about me?" Sabine asked, and they turned to her.

"Sabine, you'll need to stay here with your people," Michael answered, then held up a hand. "Not because you aren't worthy to join us, you are. But because you need to recover from everything you've seen today, and we need to focus on taking out the Duke. That's not something you can help with right now."

"May I?" Akio interrupted, and Michael nodded. Akio turned to Sabine. "I have a small communicator that will allow you to reach us. If something goes wrong again—if there's another attack or we need to touch base with you—it can be used. It does not have infinite power, so use it sparingly." He turned to Eve and asked, "We do have one in the container, yes?"

"We do," she agreed.

Akio turned back to Sabine. "For now, your job is to stay and protect, connect with your family, and work through the events of this last day. We won't be that far away."

"Japan," Sabine retorted, "at least from what I know, is damned far away."

"Yes, but Akio and I won't be in Japan," Michael said. "I don't think William is going to leave Europe."

"Why not?" Mark asked.

"Who's William?" Sabine asked.

"I suspect that William is the man you're calling the Duke," Michael answered and nodded towards Lilliana. "I've seen what he looks like from our Alpha here." He turned to Mark. "He was always an aristocrat lover, playing the political game until I caught him abusing his powers."

"What did he do?" Yuko asked.

Michael's face went dark. "He was taking the blood from people who didn't have a clue about him, and abusing them. You would call it a date rape drug." He looked around. "Okay, I have no idea what you would call it since I doubt those drugs are around anymore."

"You didn't kill him?" Sabine pressed.

Michael's face was annoyed. "Obviously not, or we wouldn't be having this discussion right now," he said. "I punished him by shutting him up in a crypt and blocking it. I expected him to take decades to die, a fitting punishment for those ladies who would have to live their lives with the scars from his abuse. He would live long enough to regret ever hurting them and as they finally passed away, so would he."

"How did he survive?" Eve asked.

"I've no idea, although I could make an educated guess that the nanites in his system must have damped it down, allowing him to hibernate far longer than I would have supposed." He looked over at Sabine. "I'll make sure to kill him permanently this time."

"So," Akio asked, "are you good with our plan, Sabine?"

She turned to him and smiled a little. "Can we negotiate for another thousand rounds of ammunition?"

"What are you thinking we need to do?" Mark asked. He was excited about going to Japan, but his concern for Jacqueline's feelings was front and center.

She smiled wistfully at Michael and Akio as they started walking Sabine back to the resistance group. "We go to Japan." She shrugged. "Michael never said he would protect me forever, and I have to admit that the fighting, what little the old bald-headed bastard allowed me, was enough for now."

She stopped when Michael turned his head and glanced at her, reaching up to touch his ear.

"Who apparently has goddamned super-hearing," she whispered before speaking louder, "Love you, Michael!" He smirked and turned his head back. "Why am I always sticking my foot in my mouth?"

Mark, watching the two men, answered truthfully. "You're passionate in your feelings and have almost zero ability to filter what comes out."

Jacqueline gazed at him, but his thoughts were elsewhere. Her eyes narrowed, but her voice was sweet. "So, the ability to filter is because I'm too slow?"

Mark's mouth opened to speak, but then he clamped it shut as he turned to look at her. "Oh no you don't!" He shook his head. "I answered truthfully, and now you're twisting my damned words. Why?"

Jacqueline's annoyance was plain on her face. Mark waited and watched as she flipped a hand. "Probably because occasionally girls are very needy emotionally; we need constant approval. Since guys are usually very guarded with their answers, we seek to confirm them in the most efficient way possible."

"By luring us into a verbal trap and springing it?"

"No, by checking your answer appropriately when your guard is down." She paused a moment, then smirked. "We create traps and spring them on you when we're pissed about other things and just want a target. I'll try not to do that to you." She thought back to the times she had argued with her dad as a teenager. "I'll try pretty hard," she amended.

Mark reached around her shoulder. "I'll try to damp down my lust for all things tech, and give you time."

"At least tech doesn't have a nice rack or sashay as she walks away." Jacqueline replied.

Mark looked out over the horizon, ready to get out of this horrible place. "No, but it doesn't say 'I have a headache' when it's plugged in, either."

Yuko snorted when Jacqueline punched him.

"Or pummel me when I just speak the truth," Mark grunted, holding his stomach.

Kirk, James and Timothy were the first three out of the building as they started towards the people coming in their direction. Kirk looked up and noticed that two guys had their rifles aimed in Michael, Akio and Sabine's direction. He turned to Timothy and asked, "Can you make sure those two assholes up there pull their guns back? I don't want to discuss things with someone who's unnecessarily antsy." Kirk turned back to look up at the top of the building. "Or have to listen to someone moan when we pull a rifle out of their ass."

Timothy turned and jerked his head at Alan, who peeled off and jogged over to the other building. Kirk looked at him, and Timothy smiled. "I'm on to you, Kirk. James is related, so if I'm gone, you're good if Sabine wants a guy."

James laughed as Kirk argued with Timothy. "I'm not trying to keep you and Sabine apart!" The laughter from those behind them had Kirk realizing it didn't matter what he said. "Fine, keep up the fantasy."

A couple of minutes later, they were close. Kirk watched Michael's easy walk and was a bit jealous of the fit of the coat, the weapons on his hips, and the sword on his back. Kirk had to admit that his full head of hair beat Michael's chrome dome though.

"Thank you," he got out, holding his hand to shake. First to Michael, then Akio, who pointed to Sabine, who was surprised and reached out to shake his hand.

"Yes," Kirk agreed and smiled at Sabine. "You too." She was embarrassed by the attention, he could tell, but she didn't seem at all uneasy about how the weapons and holsters fit. From what they knew, she'd only been using them for twenty-four hours. But he sure as hell wasn't going to get into a shooting match with her.

"Thank you," Michael replied. "Sabine is going to stay here with you, since this is where she was headed before she decided to join us last night." That got a snort from Sabine and a slight smile from Akio. "She'll need to rest, and there could be some emotional damage from our fight."

"Damage?" James said.

"Yes," Michael agreed.

THE DARKEST NIGHT

Timothy interjected, "People were killed."

"They were only Weres." A guy with brown hair commented from the back.

Sabine's eyes turned flint-hard. "And I have a Were friend. Would you like to meet her?" she asked, her anger showing on her face.

He raised his hands and Kirk came to his defense. "Remember, we hadn't met a good Were," he nodded to Michael, "or vampire, no offense intended."

Michael nodded. "None taken."

Kirk returned his gaze to her. "For *years*, Sabine. It could take us a while to come to grips with it."

Sabine nodded her understanding and added, "Sorry, I'm a little overwhelmed and still feeling twitchy."

"That will go away," James told her.

"No," Akio interrupted, "it probably will not." As they turned to him, he added. "She has seen much battle right now, and I believe she has changed, period. She ran for miles from the Weres last night. She doesn't have a bone in her body that is willing to quit. I doubt that she will change from this new Sabine."

"Okay," Sabine thought a moment. "That's both scary and rather cool."

Kirk turned to Timothy and raised an eyebrow. Timothy silently mouthed back, "I'm not quitting."

19

YUKO CLOSED THE DOOR AFTER EVE, JACQUELINE AND MARK entered the container. She turned to the two additions. "You will be able to drop seats from the sides there," she pointed left, then right, "or over there." She was pleased when the two took seats next to each other.

Young love was so beautiful. She turned to Eve, who shook her head. "What?"

Eve smiled. "It is nice to see the change in your willingness to fight after all these new adventures."

"I was not unwilling to fight," Yuko interrupted. "I was unwilling to kill. I've told you how many times? My job was to be a *diplomat*."

Mark asked, "Did it drive Akio crazy?"

Eve answered, "Not so much crazy, as it increased his concern that she would try to talk her way out of a situation where immediate action was warranted."

"That is because Akio is very quick to judge when violence is warranted."

"And we," Jacqueline asked, circling her finger to indicate everyone present, "just left him with *Michael*?"

Mark snickered.

"It's not like Michael isn't already slipping into old patterns," Eve replied. "We have data from his time in the old United States. If a situation required him to get involved, then he usually left a massive path of death."

"Those assholes needed a little killing," Jacqueline responded. "I was there, and I can tell you the world is a better place."

"It could be," Eve answered. "I'm just saying that Akio isn't going to change Michael's predilection for fast and fatal response."

"I wasn't suggesting Akio was going to change Michael's style," Jacqueline argued. "I'm suggesting that what little hesitation Akio had before is going to disappear around Michael."

"It will be like two kids in one of those candy stores I always hear about." Mark agreed.

"You hear about?" Yuko asked.

"Sure." Jacqueline shrugged. "Not much candy in the city-states in the US. I suppose there are candy stores, but I've never been in one."

"Oh." Yuko waved a hand. "Then we will remedy that tonight."

Mark's eyes widened. "Tonight?"

Jacqueline turned to him. "Didn't we tell you?"

Mark looked sideways at her, his eyes narrowing. "No. Somehow in the short amount of time since we got on this craft, you've made plans, and the guy is the last to know."

"You should get with the program," Eve replied.

"What program?" Mark asked, exasperated. "And are we going to leave any time soon?" He lifted his left arm and pretended to smell under it. "Because I smell kinda ripe."

"Not *kinda*." Jacqueline said. "You are ripe."

"We have been in the air for more than five minutes," Eve answered.

Gerard exited a second time and glanced around to see if

there was anyone in the vicinity. He listened for a moment but heard nothing, so he left the small church and walked towards the next building. The front door of this one had been ripped off and left on the floor. Stepping over the door, Gerard took the stairs to the top of the building. He wasn't up there for more than a couple of minutes when he saw a large container box rise above the buildings and head almost straight up into the atmosphere.

Gerard spat to the side. He glanced one more time at the sky, then turned around and went back down. It took only a moment to listen again, then return to the little old church and make his way back to the last room. He pushed aside the old shelf and slipped into the crevice. Using handholds probably worked into the wood centuries before, he moved the shelf back into place.

He took a small glowing ball from his pack and used it to illuminate his way through the passages. Due to the Duke's blood enhancements, he made short work of the trip to the minor passageway. On arrival, he reached up and unhooked the small latch that disengaged the trap set in the passageway. Twenty more paces and he rearmed the trap, then took off at a slight jog. The skulls seemed to laugh at him as he passed.

The one vampire the Duke had been trying to hide from was here. Gerard didn't know how Akio had figured out the plan or exactly how he had taken out the packs.

But they knew enough about that meddlesome pain-in-the-ass to know he probably had technology left over from his bitch queen that he used to stop the attacks.

The Duke was not going to be pleased when Gerard woke him.

Michael and Akio walked a quarter mile from the humans after leaving Sabine behind. The black x-wing Pod came down out of the sky as Michael turned to Akio. "Backseat?"

Akio grinned. "I usually use the front, but I'm not sure it really matters."

"Nah," Michael said as the canopy started rising, "I'm pulling your leg."

Both men pulled off their weapons and stowed them in the ship. Akio slipped into the front seat. "Where do you think he is?"

"Somewhere down in the catacombs, behind a shit-ton of traps."

"Yes, vampires are somewhat diligent about being found when they sleep in the daytime."

"True," Michael agreed.

Akio whispered some commands to Eve, and the ship started to rise. He turned his head slightly. "Did you start that?"

"I don't remember," Michael said. "I probably did some of that in my youth, but we all, human or not, tried to be safe back then. It wasn't the best time in the world to be running around anyway. Everyone took precautions."

"So, we need to consider what a multiple-century-old vampire might use to protect his lair from you?" Akio asked.

"You would have to believe your adversary was specifically me to be effective; only David ever caught *me*."

"Bethany Anne didn't give any explanation when she and John were talking about it that one time," Akio said.

Michael allowed the comment to marinate a moment before responding. "Let's just say I never gave her any information to pass along, and I'm a bit anxious about running around in Myst sometimes. It was a rather humbling experience, to be sure." Michael stopped a moment before adding, "Rather like my hair."

"Hair?"

"Yes, as in the stuff that I lack on the top of my head?" Michael replied as they gazed over the ruins of Paris. "Ever since I came out of the Etheric, I can't grow any hair on my head, and it is *pissing me off*."

"Why?" Akio asked. His own head was clean-shaven.

"Because I looked better with hair, to be truthful." Michael said as he switched from looking out the left side of the canopy to the right. "I realize it's all ego, but I'm as fragile as the next..." Michael swallowed and tried again. "I'm as fragile..."

Both men lost it, laughing at Michael's inability to call himself fragile and keep a straight face. "Sorry. The real reason," Michael finally said, "is that I hate being bald. It's emasculating."

"Was that hard to say?" Akio asked. He pointed below. "Should we land down there?"

Michael turned to look where he was pointing. "Yes, that's a good location."

As the sun was setting, the black Pod slowly descended towards the remains of the Cathedral of Notre Dame.

INSIDE THE CATACOMBS

WILLIAM RENAUD WOKE up and opened his eyes immediately. He registered the steady pace of someone walking quickly.

Straight for his room.

He got up from the bed and grabbed his weapons. There was a quiet knock on the door, then Gerard's voice called to him.

He looked down at his watch; a candle burning in the corner was all the light he needed. "What is it, Gerard?" he asked. Then said, "You may enter."

His closest advisor opened the door and stepped in, then closed the door behind him. He turned to the Duke and spoke candidly.

"My Lord, we have a problem."

Michael watched as the lightning played across the sky. The storm clouds had rolled in as they landed, and he enjoyed the play of the light and shadow over the stonework of the old cathedral. He pulled his sword out, and unholstered one gun. Akio grabbed two swords and left his pistol in his holster.

Michael was already walking into the church as the black Pod lifted into the sky. Akio headed towards the doors of the church as Michael disappeared inside.

Akio made it into the building just before a deluge of rain started outside. He saw Michael in the middle of the church, looking around.

Akio came up beside him. Michael turned and gave him a crooked grin. "I'm just seeing what's different."

Akio turned to look at him. "From the last time you were here?"

"No, from when we built it," he replied and walked purposefully away. "Come this way. The entrance to the catacombs is over here."

A moment later, Michael asked Akio, "Feel like a game of Hide and Go Kill?"

OPERATIONS ROOM, Japan

EVE WAS WORKING on a few screens as Yuko came back in, using a towel to dry her hair. "Problems?"

"When do we not have problems?" Eve answered.

"I mean," Yuko pointed to the screens, "are there any issues with the technology?"

"Well, no." Eve said. "Although if the computers could talk, they would probably complain about how they are way out of warranty."

"Okay." Yuko folded the towel and hung it over a chair to dry. "What's going on?"

"Two of our police contacts have passed us information that there will be a gang meeting tonight between Banri's gang and Choki's."

Yuko stared at the little AI. "That doesn't matter to us. That's a police responsibility. What's the real reason they are contacting us?"

"They believe there will be Wechselbalg involved."

Yuko's eyes narrowed. "That isn't normal. Akio always responds when we get wind of something like this." She considered options. "Okay, we both now think it is a trap, right?"

"When did I say it was a trap?" Eve asked.

"When you didn't say anything and let me think. You are just as bad as Akio about trying to teach me something I learned over a hundred years ago."

"If you have learned it," Eve answered, in a half-question, half-statement, "why don't we think you understand it?"

"You know, Eve," Yuko put her hand on the shoulder of the AI. "You're my dearest friend and I love you. But I've been programming logic chains and hacking computers since before I was as tall as you are now. It is always easier to make sure that even my best friends underestimate me."

Eve seemed to be stuck in a logic problem; there were no movements from her body. It was times like this when Eve demonstrated that she was obviously not human.

Yuko shook her head. "You should really use a small percentage of your computing power to keep up some semblance of being alive."

It was a full twenty more seconds before Eve came back online and looked at her friend in shock.

"You have been out with more boys!"

Yuko stared at her friend in shock. "How did you…"

"It's logical," Eve took a step towards Yuko and stuck a finger gently into her chest, poking her each time she made a point. *Poke.* "You like boys."

"That's not abnormal," Yuko protested.

Poke. "You don't go out much with boys!" Eve continued.

"Why would I?" Yuko argued. "I always have you two around!"

Poke. "You are a shy person!"

Yuko flipped her hair out of her face, annoyed. "I'm not shy, I just like my privacy!"

Poke. "You don't like Akio's comments about your boyfriends!" Eve continued.

"What comments?" Yuko shot back. "They are judgmental assessments coming from a man who can't remember when he was two hundred years old, much less twenty!"

"And..." Eve didn't have a follow up.

"And," Yuko continued, "you were only too happy to help him find dirt!"

"That's..." Eve started before her voice softened. "That's because no one is good enough for you," Eve finally finished.

"And *that* is why it's easier to be underestimated, Eve." Yuko, also speaking softly, told her. "When you guys believe me to be a bit slow, or afraid to kill, or needing more time with swords? It is a defense mechanism for me. I don't want to have to explain myself."

Eve walked to a chair five steps away and sat down. Yuko stared at her friend, who was rocking back and forth, seemingly having an existential crisis.

Yuko moved to put a hand on Eve's back. "Are you okay?" she asked. Then considered where Eve was. "And you are sitting down."

"You mentioned using a portion of my computing power to seem real." Eve looked up. "That portion decided a person in shock—like I am—might want to sit down."

"You *never* sit down." Yuko replied, then modified it. "Well, incredibly rarely."

"I don't need to sit. My body doesn't get tired, and the position is inferior if I need to react quickly. Sitting is inefficient," Eve concluded.

Yuko looked up when she heard the clearing of a throat, to find Jacqueline and Mark at the door to the operations room. She smiled at them. "Come in."

20

JACQUELINE LOOKED AROUND THE OPERATIONS ROOM AND KNEW she had lost Mark's attention for a while. Unless she was willing to strip down in front of him. Which was, she concluded, a plausible action on her part, but she didn't want to try it unless it was absolutely necessary.

It was an unfortunate truth that Mark might choose to explore the technology over playing with her naked body. That would be a large blow to her ego, something she didn't want to deal with at the moment. Sometimes geeks were a challenge that way.

There were seven different work spaces spread out against the walls in a room about thirty feet by forty feet. It had a desk in the middle and two white boards at one end. It seemed rather large for the three people who lived in the complex.

Mark was already walking over to a desk where four computer monitors were arranged in a large rectangle.

Eve noticed Mark looking at the computer screens and the data on them, but he wasn't touching and he couldn't break anything over there without making a concerted effort. She put the chance of Mark purposely damaging something significantly lower than one percent.

Of one percent.

She smiled at that thought. Her own friend had fooled her for a hundred and fifty years. Well, probably less. However, Eve had to consider all ramifications of her logic systems.

"You don't have to do that." Yuko looked down at her.

Eve looked up. "What?"

"Work to reset all of your logic systems, and don't tell me you aren't. When you do, the systems handling your body cause your right ear to twitch twice a second."

Eve moved a hand up to her right ear. "Are you making that up?"

"You mean lying?"

"Yes."

"No."

"Good," Eve said. "Because I registered that as actual truth and I'm not sure I can deal with making that many mistakes in one night."

Yuko chuckled. "You done with your existential AI crisis?"

"Well," Eve answered after a few seconds, "about 87.7% of it, and I should be done with the rest in two minutes and twenty-five seconds if you don't confuse me anymore."

"Okay." Yuko patted her friend on the shoulder. Eve had added all sorts of features over the decades, and she could tell a lot with the sensitive sensors. Yuko walked over to Jacqueline and Mark. "Questions?"

"Yup." Jacqueline jumped in before Mark could derail her with geeky stuff. "Am I seeing a chance to go bust up a gang meeting?"

Yuko shrugged. "Either that, or an attempt to kill Akio in a trap."

Mark asked, "How would they do that?"

Eve stood and walked over to join them. "Usually they try to overcome him with violence. Twice they tried to capture Yuko and use her as bait."

"Only twice?" Jacqueline asked, surprised.

"I'm considered a noncombatant." Yuko answered. "So most bad guys don't try to actually hurt me, and no one considers me dangerous."

"Why not?" Mark asked. "Seems like you can be very dangerous."

"You heard some of the conversation, didn't you?" Jacqueline asked him, scratching his back. "Yuko hasn't been much of a fighter these last hundred and fifty years."

"That she has told us about," grumped Eve. "You can't tell now."

Yuko looked down at Eve. "Wow, emotional manipulation much, Eve?"

Eve turned to look at her. "I have to try out new methodologies to—hopefully—keep you safe." Eve looked at Yuko a minute, then a small smile played on her lips. "You didn't think I'd quit trying to protect you, did you?"

Yuko smiled. "I can wish."

Eve shook her head. "That won't happen. I was there when Bethany Anne brought you aboard, and I'll be here when Bethany Anne comes back," she said.

"Well, I'm going to be harder to protect now," Yuko told her. Mark and Jacqueline just watched them as they finished their earlier discussion.

"Because you will be in the middle of the action?" Eve calculated.

"Yes."

"Wait, you were there when Bethany Anne brought her on board?" Mark asked.

"Well, it wasn't really Eve at that time," Yuko answered him. "ADAM was my main friend. As a going-away present, he built Eve and based her powerful AI on his own code. Then, he gave the AI all of the memories he had of himself with me so I could speak about our past and not be lonely."

"That's...." Jacqueline started, but didn't finish the sentence.

"Love," Eve finished for her.

CATACOMBS UNDER OLD PARIS

"So, the Queen's Bitch should be busy in Japan for a little while," the Duke told Gerard as he hung up the phone.

Gerard considered what he'd been told. "Do you believe they will be able to kill him?"

"Of course not," the Duke sniffed. "It's only a distraction to help us get out of here."

"What if he doesn't take the bait, or what if he isn't really down here?"

William Renaud considered the question. "I am sending my apostles through the catacombs to look. If they live, or find him dead in a trap, then we are fine. If they die, we need to be out of here quickly." The Duke reached over to pull his coat off a rack in the small room that he had built under the ground. Over the years, he had stolen humans from Paris and drunk his fill. Unfortunately, that made them cautious and harder to catch. "If we have to continue running, I will conclude that my idea of 'live and let live' was unwise and I should have killed him a long time ago."

He had focused all of his attention on subjugating France and the areas around it, while keeping any evidence of himself from the humans.

No need for more of the sheep to grow fangs.

Germany was one of the most technologically sophisticated areas on the planet now. With the pre-war antigrav technology provided to them, they had rebuilt a remarkable society.

It wasn't as good as Japan's, but it was more than enough for his plans.

First he would take over Germany, then the world.

His expression changed to annoyance. It was *supposed* to be Paris first, then Germany, finally the world.

That damned Akio.

"Let me tell my children what they need to do," he said to Gerard. "I'll be back."

Gerard nodded and bowed until the Duke was out of the room. He shivered just a bit. The Duke was very close to a man while remaining a vampire. His present children were little better than ravenous monsters, but he kept them around for times like this.

Release them, and allow them to suffer should any attacks come. Early warning system, he called it.

Gerard looked around and began to clean up. If they needed to leave quickly, there would be a few things they should take.

He started packing the bag.

"I'll be a son of a bitch," Michael exclaimed when the sharpened metal rods that shot through the air where he had been a microsecond before caught his coat at the very bottom. He grated his teeth in annoyance, then produced a fine molecular edge on his hand and cut through the metal rod. He pulled his coat hem up and looked at it.

It had a quarter-inch hole punched through it. "Those cretins," he hissed as his eyes flared red. He looked back down the hallway. When the trap had been sprung, Michael had jumped ahead and Akio had jumped back.

"I got lazy," Michael admitted as he turned to Akio. He reached out and used the Etheric molecular edge to cut all the rods except the topmost.

Akio wasn't that tall.

Akio shrugged as he walked through. "I'll tell you about the time a little girl shot me in the ass with a crossbow."

Michael looked at Akio's deadpan face. "Truth?"

Akio smiled a little and nodded. "I try not to dwell on it much."

"Was this recent, or hundreds of years ago?" Michael asked.

"I would like to say when I was young, dumb and foolish," Akio said. "But the truth is it happened twenty-eight years ago over in the area that was Taiwan before the war. There was a Wechselbalg group that was pretty militaristic, and one of their people who was bent on subjugating humans rose to the top. As I took care of the leader, I didn't pay attention to the children, one of whom picked up a guard's crossbow and shot me as more of his people came running in."

Michael laughed. "Well, I appreciate the sharing and it did help." He picked up his hem to look at the hole again. "But this pisses me off. I like this coat."

"Easily fixed, Michael," Akio replied, but then he noticed Michael wasn't paying any attention to him. Akio reached out with his own senses and felt faint energy in the direction they had been heading. Only a few seconds later they heard noises as something moved quickly through the catacombs.

Coming directly for them.

"What I'm *saying*," Jacqueline stated as she pointed to the monitor displaying a map of the location, "is that there's a park across from the buildings."

"And?" Yuko asked.

"Well," Jacqueline leaned into Mark who reached up and put an arm around her shoulders, "they're looking for Akio, not a pair of lovers."

"You want us," Yuko pointed to Eve and herself, "to allow you two to get involved in a police takedown between two criminal gangs, possibly including Wechselbalg, that is most likely a trap for Akio?"

Jacqueline snorted. "Yes, and your point?"

"What would Michael say?" Eve asked.

"Did you see him," Mark asked, "have any problem with us standing in front of a few thousand hungry Wechselbalg?"

Yuko opened her mouth and then shut it. She turned to Eve. "What do you think?"

Eve shrugged. "The difference in risk between the fight they were in this morning and a fight with the criminal gangs is so large as to be laughable." Eve said. "We can always ask Akio to ask Michael."

Yuko nodded. "Do that, please."

CATACOMBS UNDER OLD PARIS

SEAN GWELVIN HAD BEEN A VERY poor policeman when he was alive. When he was serving, he had learned all the diverse ways a house could be broken into, and many places and methods to hide valuables.

It was an education in theft, so he applied his education.

To steal, that is.

For a year and a half, he policed during the day, went home and took a nap, then went out to either case a location or break into it. The last three months he was alive, his captain had actually assigned him to solve his own crimes.

Amazingly enough, he failed to find the perpetrator.

Then, he made the fateful mistake of trying to break into the Duke's house looking for treasure. Instead of treasure, he found trouble.

The deadly kind.

Sean didn't remember much about the time before he was

turned, but he sure knew about his life since. The Duke was a hard master, but remarkably fair with both his praise and his punishments.

The senses honed during his thieving days were still useful. He couldn't see anything down the hallway, but he could feel that something wasn't right.

So he stopped. He smelled the air and turned in every direction, then reached into his pocket to grab his warning device and froze. Looking down, he pulled his pocket inside out before shoving it back in and checking the other three pockets.

"Looking for this?" a man's voice asked him.

Sean twisted around, eyes flashing red, and hissed.

What he saw scared his lizard brain so much he couldn't speak.

"Akio?" a tiny voice called in his ear. Akio turned away from the distraction of Michael ripping apart the Forsaken down the hallway.

"Yes, Eve?"

"Yuko would like you to pass on a question to Michael as to whether it's okay to get Jacqueline and Mark involved in an operation."

"There?" he asked as he glanced down the hallway in time to see Michael decapitate the body and turn to look back at him. Down here, there were tiny flames every forty feet, enough that you could see decently if you were advanced.

"Yes."

Akio considered it a moment. "Tell me about it." He stayed quiet as Michael joined him. "So, a trap." he said as she finished.

"Oh, definitely." Eve agreed.

"Problems?" Michael asked.

Akio summarized Eve's communication.

"So," Michael replied, "we have two gangs, some Wechselbalg and perhaps cops involved in an attempt to capture or kill you?"

Akio gave a minute shrug. "Probably kill."

"And the two young ones wish to be a part of this to do what?"

Eve answered loud enough for Michael to hear, slightly hurting Akio's ears. "They don't like that there will be innocent cops involved."

"There's no way of knowing they're innocent," Michael said, "without Akio or me to confirm."

"In Japan," Akio offered, "look for cops firing their guns at the bad guys. That is a good enough determination because any bad cops won't be shooting." Michael raised an eyebrow, so Akio continued, "The old days where only the cops and the Yakuza had guns is gone. Too many times a Wechselbalg has rampaged as a wolf and killed indiscriminately. Now the cops have guns with silver bullets as well. While some are paid by the criminals, most are not." He shrugged. "Japan is still mostly civilized, but it is a harsh life now when someone can change into a creature that is almost impossible to kill. So, civilians have guns."

Michael nodded his understanding. "Yuko wants my permission for two adults to go into harm's way?"

There was a very faint, "That's what I told them!" coming from Akio's implant.

Michael smiled. "They're old enough to decide what to do on their own. I didn't promise them they wouldn't die in Europe, and I can't say they're safe in Japan either." He could almost see the cold water splash on Jacqueline's face when she heard those words and the narrowing of her eyes as she took on the responsibility anyway.

"However," Michael continued, "make sure they know I will be very upset with both of them if they get killed. And if I figure out a way to resurrect them, I will make them train every day for ten years so it doesn't happen again."

"Oh shit." This time it was Mark's voice.

"Yeah," Jacqueline chimed in, "that training bullshit is for the birds. So try not to die."

"Got it."

Akio smiled at the two talking in his ear. "That is all?"

"We are good," Eve agreed, and they closed the connection.

Michael rolled his eyes before turning back to Akio. "Children!" He pulled a device out of his pocket. "What do you suppose this does?"

Akio looked at Michael, who was smiling. "You already know."

21

NAGOYA, JAPAN

"OH MY GOD," Mark whispered as the four of them walked through the city of Nagoya. All the buildings had electricity and cars whisked overhead. "This is nothing like New York." His head kept swiveling, trying to take in all the sights. "How does everyone have so much here?"

"We kept them safe," Yuko answered. "Bethany Anne made a secret agreement and placed enough armaments to protect the island in case of a war. She wanted a place that Michael could come and be safe when he made it back."

Mark snorted.

Jacqueline watched a version of a motorcycle whiz past her. "They make almost no sound," she noted before asking Yuko, "Bethany Anne trusted the Japanese government?"

Yuko smiled. "Hardly."

"Why then," Jacqueline watched another motorcycle speed past, the lights underneath the fairing coloring the street. "Did she give them guns?"

"She didn't, exactly. She gave Yuko and me guns and plans. From there, we took on the responsibility to make sure those weapons were used according to the agreements we had worked out."

"They didn't try to just take them?"

"Oh, certainly." Yuko nodded and pointed for them to go across the street. "After Akio *discussed* it with them, they stopped."

"Stopped trying or breathing?" Mark asked.

"Yes." Yuko replied.

Mark was surprised to see passing vehicles come to a stop and wait for them. "The laws here are strong enough to make sure everyone stops?"

"Of course," Yuko said, but a small smile played on her face, "but that isn't the only answer."

There was a long pause before Eve spoke. "What she means is that we have multiple companies here in Japan. Interestingly enough, the most secretive is a programming group which is responsible for all upper EI capabilities, including the role-specific EIs that run all the cars, including those that can be taken over by manual control."

"Wait!" Mark came back, excited to see the cars start up again once they stepped onto the sidewalk. "You mean you wrote the code that runs these cars?"

Eve nodded. "You are very perceptive."

"Why you?" Jacqueline asked.

"Because she's the best programmer in Japan," Mark answered. "Probably the world, right?"

"Probably," Eve agreed. "I only qualify that because there is a very small chance that the EI in the Colorado base is better, but that chance is less than one in four thousand."

"Daaamnnnn," Mark whispered.

"I would never have guessed," Jacqueline said, "that I was walking around with a couple of businesspeople."

"More like business moguls, but that might be bragging." Yuko replied, and stopped. "Okay," she nodded down a street, "fifteen blocks south is the park. It is next to the port where we need to meet the police. It is about two hours before the meeting is supposed to occur. Use your implants to communicate, but remember there are supposed to be Wechselbalg here." Yuko turned to Jacqueline. "Are you able to deal with an Alpha's command?"

"Fuck," Jacqueline spat out, "I have no Alpha but Michael. They can bring it."

Mark poked her in the ribs. "What about me, baby?"

She turned and jabbed him with her elbow, then smiled. "I don't know, ask me next time and we'll see who ends up on top, okay?"

"Okay." Mark's eyes went a touch vacant. "Either way, I win."

Yuko snapped her fingers twice. "A little focus would be good here."

Jacqueline blushed. "Sorry, I'm still reacting like a wolf in heat."

"No," Yuko shook her head, "like a woman ready to pounce on her man. Just make sure you guys don't lose it out there so that Michael has to try and resurrect you."

"Can he do that?" Mark asked.

"No." Yuko said, and Mark's face lost its humor.

"Well, baby," Mark held his hand out for Jacqueline to take, "let's go to the park, shall we?"

POLICE OFFICE, Nagoya Japan

"INSPECTOR HIRANO?"

Inspector Jijo Hirano turned to the young lady and raised an eyebrow. "Yes?"

At the moment, he happened to be at the front desk of the

station instead of his own office or out on a bust that needed his oversight, and he was surprised someone knew who he was.

Especially with his back turned. She couldn't have seen his name badge. "Reporter?" he asked.

She shook her head. "I'm here to discuss something with you," she replied. "May we go to your office?"

Hirano stepped up to the counter that separated the police from the civilians and placed his hands and elbows on the five-foot-tall surface. This meant he was looking down slightly at the woman standing three feet in front of him. "Well, it all depends on what we need to talk about. I apologize, but I don't have the time to just chat about anything—"

She interrupted him. "The Bitch Protocol."

The blood left the inspector's face. "I see."

At that moment, the regular officer of the desk came back. "Thank you, sir!" he said.

The inspector barely nodded in his direction as he directed the attractive young woman to follow him to his office.

Kimio watched them leave. "Lucky bastard," he breathed, and then took his seat, waiting for the next hot young woman to come in so he could help her.

Yuko walked behind the inspector, making sure to watch him as she kept her senses alert. While Eve was fairly sure this inspector was clean, it could be that he was just very good at hiding his real affiliation.

The inspector opened his door and held it to allow Yuko to step in. She was wearing her black operations gear under a large and easily disposed of dress.

"Thank you." Yuko nodded as he closed the door.

"Well," he said as he moved to sit behind his desk, "if you are who I think you are, then it is I who needs to thank you."

Yuko turned her head. "Meaning?"

Hirano pursed his lips and opened the top drawer of his desk. He bent over to the right side and used keys to open the bottom drawer. He pulled out the book, binder really, that was kept inside and locked the drawer again. He laid the book down on his desk and ran his hand across it reverently before unfastening its bronze clasp and opening it.

Yuko was surprised to see notepapers inside, all glued or taped. Running her eyes over the first three entries on the first page, she saw they were from over five decades before.

"This book was my father's," Hirano announced. "When I found it after he died, I thought he was perhaps delusional. It wasn't until I met my first Wechselbalg that I went back to my mother's home and searched for the book. I have kept it up to date since then."

"Why paper?" Yuko asked.

Hirano grinned. "Because the wife of ADAM cannot find what isn't in the systems, can she?"

Yuko laughed a second before she slapped a hand over her mouth in surprise. "Sorry!" she said in a muffled voice. "That shocked me."

Hirano smiled. Meeting a living legend wasn't what he had expected to occur today. She was even more beautiful than the description that his father had written in the entries in the book. "That I know that Eve exists?"

"No," Yuko answered, removing her hand. "That you called her the wife of ADAM." Yuko thought about it. "Although it is accurate in a way, I suppose."

"So, Eve is absolutely real as well?" Hirano asked. "I know that I am acting as if it is true, but we didn't have proof."

"Oh, certainly, she is outside right now," Yuko answered and smiled as Hirano craned his neck, obviously wishing that he could go look. "She is not on this side of the building, Inspector."

"Oh," he turned back to Yuko. "Sorry."

"No offense taken," Yuko said, but she now understood why Jacqueline could be annoyed by Mark's attraction to technology.

This inspector was kind of cute. She would have to inform Eve that the AI had turned an inspector's head.

He continued his explanation, "It is not that I am any less impressed with you, my lady," he bowed slightly, "but she really is the ghost in the machine, is she not?"

Yuko considered that a moment. "Both machine and shell, I could argue," she said before continuing, "As much fun as this is to consider," she nodded to his book, "we have a situation going down at the port, and I am here to find out if I can trust any of the police who will be there."

"The port isn't my jurisdiction," he said and pushed his book out of the way so he could see the screen in his desktop. "Let's see who we will have working down there with you."

Ten minutes later, Hirano stuck his head out of his office and yelled, "Hana!"

"Here!" a woman's voice called as she came out of an office two doors down. Hirano gestured for her to join him and retreated into his office.

"Well," Michael breathed out, annoyed with himself, "shit."

Akio stepped over the latest severed arm, whose blood was seeping into the old limestone. It held a device in its hand.

"He got a message out?" Akio asked.

Michael looked down. "I think so," he said, then shrugged. "At least, he thought he had by the time I cut off his arm."

"That's five we've found, and all five had communications devices."

"So how do we find the roach before he leaves the nest?" Michael asked. "These passages seem different than the last time I was here."

"When was that?" Akio asked.

Michael thought about it a moment. "When I was traveling to

Paris with Bethany Anne," he said. "I swung down here for a little rest and relaxation while she was safely enjoying boxes of shoes."

Akio stared at Michael a moment. "Catacombs full of bones are restful and relaxing?"

"Well," Michael replied, "saying it that way, certainly not. But when you know the *why*, it helps."

Michael waited for Akio.

"Okay, why?" he finally asked, and Michael grinned.

"First, it wasn't shopping for shoes. Second, because the skull of a dear friend, Robespierre, was interred here. He and I had many letters back in the 1700s related to suffrage, the rights of the royalists, and other topics. In a way, it was a very violent time, and while society was growing, the changes had been very deadly."

"You spoke to skulls?" Akio asked, trying to piece together Michael's story.

"No such thing," he replied. "I merely came here to be grounded and explore honor and incorruptibility. Maximilien was a pleasant person to converse with on those subjects. The discussions about virtue and terror were particularly intense. It was during that time I was, perhaps, influenced to refine the Strictures."

To this, Akio just nodded. The harshness of the Strictures now made more sense.

"Eve?" Akio said and then listened a moment. "Yes, I understand. Do we have anything that might track traffic from Paris?" He waited a moment more before adding, "Okay, let's see what we can do."

"Nothing?" Michael asked.

"She says the cloud cover will cause a problem. However, she will review the next six hours of video when she gets back from the operation to see if there are any vehicles that could have come from this area."

"She'll backtrack, then?" Michael asked, and Akio nodded.

"Well," he pointed down a path, "let's see if we can find anything else."

"Find anything or anyone?" Akio asked, looking at the dead Forsaken on the ground.

"Yes," Michael replied.

Near the Port, Nagoya, Japan

THE TWO BUILDINGS each stood five stories tall, like two decorative columns flanking the street that passed between them. It continued to the port's gate five blocks distant. The park across the street from the buildings was pleasant. Occasionally ocean smells would assault those enjoying themselves, but not often. The Nagoya Port wasn't close to the sea itself, but rather was located on Ise Bay. The bay opened onto the Philippine Sea and didn't have the same surface area for the winds to pick up scent.

"You realize," Mark was busy kissing Jacqueline's neck, "that just twelve hours ago, we were in Europe kicking ass."

Jacqueline moaned. "Don't you mean watching ass being kicked?" she asked. "Stop that, I'm not paying attention like I should!" Mark stopped the kissing. "You idiot!" She jerked an elbow into his stomach. "Don't listen to me!"

Mark chuckled and thought to himself, *Mark 1, Jacqueline 0.*

Jacqueline asked, "Is that a pistol I feel, baby, or are you happy to see me?" A second later she added, "sorry, too big, never mind."

Mark 1, Jacqueline 1.

Four hover cars glided out of the evening sky, keeping their speed down to appropriate levels, and settled a foot above the road a quarter mile from the two warehouses. The four sets of headlights Banri had noticed in front of them that were landing some distance away on the road should be Choki's group.

The port did not allow anyone to overfly their airspace, on pain of missiles tearing up the offender's ass.

"It is a shame," Banri commented, "that this meeting is being held under temporary partnership."

Banri's right-hand woman Eriko said nothing, but his third, Osamu, spoke up. "It would be nice to send a few rounds in their direction."

Eriko glanced over at Osamu. He did not make eye contact with her, but his lip turned up in the annoying way that said, "Scored one with the boss!"

Their car slowed down and parked next to the building, two parked closer to the other building, and the last slid behind them. They never placed the boss in the same car twice in a row. For this trip he was in the first car, but for the next trip? It hadn't been decided yet.

The four cars they had seen coming up the road parked beside the building as they had expected. One of them, a van, pulled up in front.

Banri frowned, and Eriko whispered, "Good choice, we shall do the same next time."

Banri's frown softened. "*Hai.*"

Osamu's black eyes glinted in frustration. Eriko showed no smile, but inside she was mentally using a foreign hand gesture to tell him to go fuck himself.

She would take out her frustration on him the next time they sparred.

When the teams got out, Banri was perplexed at the eight that got out of Choki's van.

Eriko turned to look around and whispered in his direction, "The *gaijin* are the wolves our contact said would come and help with Akuryō."

Banri grunted his understanding. "Do you have support in place?" She nodded. "Good. There is no 'help' to kill Akuryō. We will do as we have been paid to, and then we leave to let the others suffer Akuryō's wrath."

Eriko agreed.

Banri buttoned his suit coat and walked towards Choki, who was coming towards him with his second and a *gaijin*. They would meet in the middle of the street. This was a weekend, and at this time of the day there was little traffic at this location.

The two men met and bowed as courtesy demanded. "What do we see here?" Choki asked, and Banri turned sideways to look at his second. Eriko said, "A *gaijin* couple necking in the park, and five police watching us."

Choki's second nodded and the *gaijin* agreed.

Both men thought a moment. "If we are not attacked, or if Akuryō should make an appearance, we separate in peace per the agreement," Choki said as he looked around.

Banri nodded. "Agreed."

"Is there anything special about the couple in the park?" Eriko asked. The *gaijin* next to Choki turned towards the park and sniffed. "I can't smell anything, and they have been here a little while according to a flyby we did thirty minutes ago. So, if they are *kaibutsu*, then they must be Wechselbalg, not vampire."

Banri thought it funny that his own team had done two flybys rather than just the one. Three hours ago the couple wasn't there, and forty-five minutes ago they were. Either way, the couple could be a plant by Akuryō's group, or just two people wishing to have some time to themselves.

Poor choice to stay and neck, but that wasn't his problem. While Japanese law looked down on stray bullet kills—a stricture left over from before the war—when Wechselbalg were involved, almost all gunfire deaths, provided they weren't intentional, were viewed much more generously.

There were no vampires on Japanese soil who didn't answer to Akuryō. If a vampire showed up and was willing to work with the Yakuza, it wouldn't be too long before that vampire disappeared and stories of Akuryō would be whispered once more.

Banri was starting to think that perhaps Akuryō was a fiction created by the police to explain clandestine murder and provide a scapegoat.

He hadn't quite finished his thoughts when the shooting started.

22

FRANCE

THE AIRCAR SLIPPED out of the ravine and headed across the country to the north. There were two people inside: the driver, and the passenger in the back seat. It was quiet in the vehicle for a few minutes.

William Renaud played with his small video device. "Be careful, Gerard," he said crisply. "We don't want to get too far outside the beam, or we lose… Damn." He played with the device. "Turn us back around. How far away are we now?"

"We are just over two hundred kilometers, sir."

"That's good. Move us back a bit and see if there is a location where we can rest and hide."

It took Gerard another five minutes to locate the ruins of an old city where he could safely tuck their vehicle into a broken up parking garage on the second-to-top floor. It was high enough to receive the signal well, and hidden from view above.

Anyone who had heard about the Queen's Bitch knew he used superior airships. There were many stories of those who sought to kill him so they could take his technology. Obviously, since he was alive, it meant those others were not.

William had no illusions that the people he had hired in Japan were going to survive. That was merely the price of business. He offered a deal, they accepted. It was how business had been done for centuries.

Now he had proof someone was searching the catacombs, but he had not received notification that anyone had been killed. Therefore, his people were down. He reached over to his own controller and tapped in the request to his people.

He received two responses. He thought about this for a second and sent a rare command, one he had taught his people after they changed, but had never used. Only one response came back.

He hoped this worked.

"Let's make sure we don't lose this signal, Gerard," he said as he looked at the video.

"Well, that was interesting," Michael said as he held up the device.

"You sent the response indicating that everything is okay?" Akio guessed.

"Yes, but it came back with another signal, and I hadn't lifted that one from any of their minds," Michael said. "So now he knows that one, if more than one alive, is fake." Michael dropped the device and crushed it under his foot. "I hate it when a plan doesn't come together."

Akio smirked, then turned to listen to the nearest hallway. "Running."

Michael smiled, then he and Akio were in Myst form. They floated down hallways trying to locate the sound as it echoed through the catacombs.

JAPAN

"INSPECTOR HIRANO," Yuko pointed to the small video feed her drone was sending to the Inspector's car, "those *gaijin* are Wechselbalg."

The inspector nodded and reached for his own communication device. He picked it up and spoke into it. "Inspector Tabata, this is Inspector Hirano."

A moment later a voice came over the line, "My apologies Inspector, we're having a bit of a moment here."

"If you mean you are firing your weapons at Banri and Choki and a number of Wechselbalg, I would say you are right to call it a *moment*."

"We have the superior position, weapons and defenses. We will be fine," the other inspector replied, annoyed.

"You are going to be dying momentarily if you don't—" He was speaking when the communication stopped.

"Too late," Yuko said, sadness in her voice.

"There are more than five up there, Choki!" Daven growled, then he ripped off his shirt. The silver slug that had hit his shoulder hurt horribly. He grabbed a knife and dug it out as he ran towards the building. With the slug gone, he changed into a wolf and joined his brethren.

Akiro Sugita contemplated the other seven people at the windows there on the fourth floor as they fired on the werewolves below. "More firepower!" he yelled, then rushed to the back of the fortified room that was at least half the size of the whole floor. Officer Satow joined him, and they ripped off the cover of the rocket-propelled gun.

"Anyone?" Sugita asked in a hurried whisper.

Satow looked over his shoulder. "No."

"Damn Inspector Tabata, if he hadn't changed the plans…" Sugita growled as he flipped the arming on, stood up and made sure there wouldn't be a backblast problem, and pulled the trigger.

Those outside saw the fourth floor of the building explode outward.

"I think that gunfire is our signal," Jacqueline said, but a voice in her ear responded, "Stand down, Inspector Hirano is calling the shots."

"The shots," Mark answered, hearing Yuko in his own ear, "are being shot already!"

"Nevertheless," Yuko answered, "we are under the… One moment."

The line went dead while the pair got up and found shelter behind a large statue. "Damn, that's a lot of shots."

The explosion on the fourth floor of the building caught them by surprise. Both ducked behind the statue as debris rained down around them.

Moments later, they could hear new sirens coming in from behind them.

"Mission approved," Yuko spoke into their ears. "Capital punishment has been authorized."

"Fuck!" Jacqueline frowned as she kicked off her boots. "That's the only outcome I was ever taught."

"That's kind of…" Mark was searching for a phrase when he finally gave up, shrugged his shoulders, and said, "Michael."

She turned and grabbed him for a kiss, then winked. "Hell yeah that's Michael." She nodded over her shoulder as the wolves howled behind them and the sirens got closer. "What say we go and do unto them as Michael would?"

The female police officer eyed the two from her own force who killed her friends. "You dead dogs," Sergeant Miyu Tao whispered as she rolled onto her side. Her ribs felt cracked, at the least, from the blast concussion that had thrown her up against the far wall. So far, neither Sugita nor Satow had looked in her direction. She unholstered her weapon and shot twice in quick succession.

Both men dropped, bullets having passed through their skulls.

She coughed up blood and spat it out. Crawling over to the massive opening in the wall, she peeked out and then started shooting. A moment later another of her team made it, and the two lone guns fired down on those below.

"Who the fuck are they?" Choki pointed to the two *gaijin* who were walking around the statue. Neither looked at all intimidated by the gunfire or bothered by the police vehicles screaming down from the sky.

"What?" Banri yelled. The two gang leaders had taken shelter behind Banri's car, which was now full of bullet holes.

"The lovers?" Choki said, wondering.

That's when the woman changed forms and became a walking myth.

"Dammit!" Banri spat. How the hell had Akuryō found a Pricolici to attack them? "She can still be hurt by silver and guns!" he yelled. He was about to turn to Eriko and order her to attack them when he saw the man's eyes light up in red fire.

Fuck this shit. "*Retreat!*" he yelled and grabbed Choki. "Vampire!" He pointed back to the lovers, but all he saw was the Pricolici running at the wolves, roaring. He twisted around. "Where the *hell* did the vampire go?"

Daven turned when he heard the Alpha challenge, his hackles rising. All the wolves turned with him, their attack momentarily forgotten as the roar overcame Daven's response.

"I ammm the bittchhh yoouu fearrr!" Jacqueline howled as she slammed into the wolves, ripping through them. When she

201

finally stopped and turned around half a block later, she casually twisted the head from the snarling wolf she was holding and dropped the body next to her.

"Everyone focus on that wolf-woman…" Banri's gurgled last words were lost as Mark pulled his clawed hand out of Banri's back. "I would have used a sword," Mark hissed in the dying man's ear, "but this seemed a bit more enjoyable." His red eyes took in the people who were now staring at him in fear. "*No one*," he screamed, "will target my woman!"

Daven knew it was a lost cause as he raced towards the towering Pricolici, but this was his only hope. Attack her and then sprint away and get lost in the port, hoping that she would stay to fight.

He dashed at her, but she didn't seem worried. Didn't even seem to prepare as he feinted a bite to her groin, then went for her hamstring. His muzzle was met with a knee, which smashed cartilage and bone. He bounced to the side but still had enough in him to shake it off and continue his flight towards the port.

Yuko commanded, "*Down!*"

The car went down. She didn't bother to let it settle to a stop, but threw open the door and jumped the last ten feet. The disposable dress had already been torn off and the young-looking woman landed, dressed all in black. She pulled one of her personal Jean Dukes out of its holster and casually shot the wolf that was running away in the back of the head.

She *had* considered shooting it in the ass, but it probably wouldn't kill the wolf and she didn't want any to get away.

She pulled the other gun, and then bodies started exploding. No more was she going to be known as the diplomat.

That was the past.

Twice, she didn't shoot when the Yakuza members dropped their weapons and started to raise their hands, but none of the Wechselbalg survived. Those that she had not personally killed or put out of the fight, Jacqueline obliterated. Within moments, the silence on the street was enveloping. Even the sirens had been turned off. The red lights flickered on the darkened buildings; the sun was almost down.

Jacqueline growled as she walked up to her, and Yuko turned to see one of the police officers looking at her with his hand on his holstered weapon. "If you darrree pulll thatt gunnn," Jacqueline ground out, "I willl ripp yourrr spine oouut yourrr asssss."

"Sawa!" Inspector Hirano snapped. "Get your hand off your pistol or I'll shoot you myself."

Yuko's red eyes started to return to normal. "You have two, maybe three alive on the fourth floor up there." She nodded to the destroyed area.

The inspector snapped out commands as Mark jogged past them calling out, "I'll help them get up there!"

Yuko nodded and turned to the inspector as she holstered her weapons.

"My stories," he remarked, looking around before returning his gaze to her, "have always had you as a diplomat?"

Paris Catacombs

MICHAEL AND AKIO worked out how to use their separate hearing to triangulate better, finding the last Forsaken as he ran down a small hallway that opened into another room. Michael stopped and reappeared as the Forsaken literally ran into the two older vampires.

Nothing but pieces of the body went past them.

The two men turned as one to see the decapitated, armless body stagger before it fell. Michael turned to Akio. "You need to speed up a little. One slice?"

Akio's eyes narrowed and a small smile played at the edge of his lips.

They looked around. Michael went left, Akio went right. A few moments later, Michael heard, "Door!"

He came back around from his hallway and walked over to Akio.

"You're right," Michael agreed. "Door."

Akio tried rolling his eyes again. "Keep that up," Michael encouraged. "You can express so much more with body language than you have so far. Your ability to stay as motionless as a mannequin is preternatural."

Akio didn't take the bait. "Trap?"

Michael cocked his head and reached up, stopping just before he reached the top. He lowered his hand again. "Probably not."

"Why?" Akio asked.

Michael jerked a thumb over his shoulder. "I'm thinking the tumbling Forsaken here would have tripped it. He didn't seem particularly bright."

Akio thought about that a moment. "What if he was supposed to trip it and catch us in here?"

"Yes, I considered that angle, but gave the other a one-percent higher chance."

"I'll go with trap."

Michael considered the door to the next room and disappeared. Akio heard in his mind, *I figured you would.*

The room behind the door was very clean. There were still a couple of lights burning. He reached out and felt four small electronic pulses, but nothing that felt like explosives.

He appeared in the middle of the room and waited.

Nothing.

Michael shrugged, walked over to the door, turned the knob, and opened it.

JAPAN

YUKO CONSIDERED her answer before replying to the inspector. "I *am* considered the diplomat. That was the role I embraced in the past."

"And now?" Inspector Hirano asked.

"Now I'll be known as a diplomat when I occasionally seek out peaceful solutions compared to others."

"Akuryō?" The Inspector asked, "or is it Akio?"

Yuko raised an eyebrow. "Well, it is Akio," she admitted. "Although he might be considered a diplomat now as well."

This time it was the inspector whose brows raised. Yuko watched the short figure emerge from the trees at the back of the park. She scanned the surrounding area, noticing one of the Wechselbalg Jacqueline had fought starting to twitch. "Inspector?"

"Hmm?" he asked, looking towards her.

"Do you have any silver handcuffs?"

"Of course, but we never use them," he said. "I have no idea if they will work."

She put a hand out. "Let me see them."

The Inspector turned to his left. "Wataru," he called. "Wechselbalg cuffs!"

A moment later the uniformed officer brought a heavy pair of cuffs and handed them to Yuko, who turned and tossed them to someone on the other side of the inspector.

He turned and was surprised to see a young girl, or short woman, next to him. It took him a moment. "Eve?"

The young woman looked up at him. "Have we met?"

"No." He held out his hand. "Inspector Hirano."

"Eve," she replied and shook his hand. She turned to Yuko. "Where?"

Yuko gestured over her shoulder. "There is a Wechselbalg that Jacqueline left alive."

Eve nodded and started walking towards the building.

"Um," the inspector licked his lips, "will she be okay?"

"Eve?" Yuko smiled. "Of course, why?"

"She's so tiny," he replied, looking past Yuko.

"Don't let that fool you," she said. "She is much stronger than she looks."

"How do you know those cuffs will work?"

"You bought them from one of our companies," Yuko confided. "Your precinct didn't cheap out. There is a number that lets us know the tested strength of the cuffs."

"So, they will hold a Wechselbalg?"

"Well," Yuko temporized, "they wouldn't hold someone like Jacqueline, but they're good for any of the other Wechselbalg that were involved."

"I heard that!" a young woman's voice called and they turned to see a woman breaking off from a group of officers who had at least five of the Yakuza in cuffs. Those had been the criminals around Mark when Yuko had started shooting. "I'm not planning on testing them for you."

She was coming right at them, and the inspector had to swallow down a bit of fear. Wechselbalg were bad enough, with their ability to change into wolves and shrug off bullets. Here he was talking with a myth; a Were who walked upright.

Not like Yuko wasn't a bigger myth, actually.

Jacqueline caught up with them and Yuko made the introductions. Once again, the inspector shook hands rather than bow. Yuko appreciated that he seemed capable of jumping back and forth between regional customs.

"Inspector?" a voice called, and Hirano turned around. The young man who had hailed him held out a communicator.

"A moment, ladies?" he asked, and walked towards the vehicle.

The two women turned to see a large white vehicle, blue lights flashing, arriving from the city.

"Ambulance," Yuko told her.

"I was wondering when that was going to happen," Jacqueline replied. "I'm pissed they held us back so long."

"You would not have been able to stop the killing among the police," Yuko said. "Did you know that the police had someone in their midst who would kill their own people?"

"Um," Jacqueline thought a moment.

"We had doubts, but we didn't *know*, did we?" Yuko pointed out.

"No," she said finally as the inspector walked back to them.

"So," the inspector asked, "are we all going to forget this occurred?"

Yuko smiled at the all-knowing, all-*guessing*, inspector. "Not right now."

"Akio?" he asked.

"Only if someone up in the chain makes a special request, I would think," she replied.

"Why? Is that what they did when my dad's memory was wiped?" he asked.

"Nooo…" she said, thinking back to the large research book the inspector had. "That was Akio's typical method of keeping us hidden."

"So why won't he do it again?" asked Hirano. "I have two diary entries where my dad put down he had met you two, then later thought he must have dreamt it."

There was a scuffle behind them, and they turned to watch. "Let me be!" a male Wechselbalg, handcuffed, yelled at Eve. He stood a good two feet taller than her.

Eve promptly kicked out and smashed his kneecap, then swiped his legs from under him. He slammed to the ground and soon had Eve's hand pointing rudely right in his face. He tried to bite her finger, and the loud crack of her slap made the inspector wince.

"He will heal in a few minutes like it never happened," Yuko commented. "Violence is the only mode of communication some Wechselbalg understand."

"Tell me about it," Jacqueline agreed.

The next time Eve pulled the man up, he didn't yell. The three turned back to each other to continue the conversation.

"Where was I?" Yuko asked. "Oh yes. We won't be removing any of your memories unless those above you care to have it done, and I doubt they will this time."

"Why this time?" he asked.

"Because we are going to become more active and change a few of our procedures, I believe," she said.

"Why?"

"Well, I could tell you," Yuko smiled, then looked around, "but it would need to be someplace a little more private than here, Inspector."

"I heard that!" Eve called to Yuko. The inspector looked at the ladies. Yuko rolled her eyes. The one called Jacqueline covered her mouth, but from the glint in her eyes she was laughing.

23

PARIS CATACOMBS

MICHAEL PULLED OPEN the door and stood aside. "Do come in."

Akio nodded and stepped inside. "Someone's private residence while they are down here?"

"I think so too," Michael said as they looked around.

"I'll be damned," William whispered as he watched the man appear in his video. "You were dead when I got out, I made sure to find out."

Gerard couldn't quite make out the Duke's comment. "Sir?"

"Nothing, Gerard." He spoke louder, "I see the answer to a question, and the fates have provided me with the means of revenge this time."

William didn't usually tell his enemy his plans before he implemented them. Perhaps if he didn't have a choice between execution of the plan or lording it over Michael he might have been tempted.

Execution won. He reached over to a second device and started punching in a code.

A moment later, he pressed a button.

The muffled multi-directional explosions caught both Akio and Michael by surprise. They bolted out of the room as Michael yelled, "Meet you back here!"

Then he disappeared.

JAPAN

THE LAST TWO police cars were sitting on the side of the street. The officer didn't want to interrupt the inspector, but they had finished everything. It was now close to three in the morning, and he had noticed both the young man and woman yawning. Hell, *he* had been yawning.

He walked up to the inspector and asked, "Time to go?"

Thankfully, the inspector didn't seem upset. "We have everything, inspector," he said.

"Okay." Hirano turned back, but didn't get to say anything before Yuko spoke up.

"Do you need a ride somewhere?" she asked.

"Yes, please," he said, before he realized that Eve had just looked at Yuko with annoyance.

Yuko turned to the officer. "Thank you, we will make sure the inspector gets home safely."

He nodded and left.

No way was the officer telling her that the inspector was supposed to go back with them.

"You," Eve spoke quietly, too softly for the human inspector to hear them, "are doing this to tweak me!" Jacqueline was having a hard time keeping a straight face.

"Is it bothering you?" Yuko asked, just as quietly.

"Are you that into him?" Eve shot back.

"No, Eve." Yuko replied. "I'm not doing this to tweak you." A moment went by before Yuko asked, "Did you know he and his father have a research folder on us, and he was trying to get a glimpse of you earlier today at the police station?"

Eve turned in confusion as they walked through the park. "There are no files on any of us. I constantly make sure of that."

"There can be," Yuko answered, "when all the information is on paper."

"Paper," Eve spat, "is one of the most annoying storage mediums on this planet."

"That's because you can't hack it," Mark said.

"Who asked you, Vamp-Nerd?" Eve asked.

"I believe," Jacqueline said a moment later, "that would be Vamp-Geek, wouldn't it?"

"Annoying," Eve clarified and then closed her eyes a moment before opening them and saying, "I've just become Akio."

Michael was already standing outside the room they had found when Akio returned. "Three hallways, all blocked."

"Three my way, the same." Michael agreed.

"Myst?" Akio asked.

"Possible," Michael answered, "although I doubt it. The workmanship seemed very good and upgraded. Almost like someone wanted to get some revenge. Turnabout is fair play and all that."

"He thought you would come?" Akio asked.

Michael waved a hand. "I doubt he thought about it consciously. But I made it very unlikely he would ever be able to leave his prison, so maybe he was subconsciously trying to best what I had accomplished?"

"How is just shutting us in besting us?"

"Well..." Michael broke off as a voice from the other room caught their attention.

"Hello, Michael, it's William. I can hear you two talking out in the hall. Why not come in here where we can chat more easily?"

Michael raised his voice. "I think not, William. You don't expect this to hold me, do you?"

"Only long enough," William replied.

"I'll bite," Michael answered before grimacing. "I can't believe I just said that."

Akio nodded. "Bad pun."

"You two can continue the fun-and-games routine," William said from the room, "but you might want to practice holding your breath. Goodbye, Michael. I do hope you pass away in a spectacularly painful fashion."

"Eve!" Akio shouted, but Michael shook his head.

"Not yet," he replied to Akio.

"Why not?" Akio asked.

"Because we haven't tried hard enough yet. Plus, we have time," Michael said as another thump of explosives sounded. There was a small rumbling, then a larger crash that caused both men to look around in alarm.

"That, gentleman," William said, his voice barely audible over the rapidly rising noise. "Is the River Seine coming to cradle your dead bodies in her bosom. I can't claim to have built most of these traps. I just found them, and perhaps added a few modifications to make them deadlier."

Michael pursed his lips. "Well, fuck." He turned to Akio. "Don't suppose you have a technological way out of this one?"

Akio slowly shook his head. "For what it is worth," he replied, "Eve could not have gotten here quickly enough."

"I do so love to hear your witty dialogue," William said.

Michael turned towards the room and stepped in. "Oh, hello Michael..." The static was immediate when Michael tossed energy throughout the room.

"I hope that broke his eardrums," Michael said as he walked back out of the room. "Now, let's see if I can reverse my last trip to the Etheric with a modicum of ability."

The water started sweeping into the room. *"Gott Verdammt!"* he spat. "I'm not getting my coat wet!" Michael opened himself up to his anger, something that seemed always to reside just below the surface of his calm thoughts, and traveled beyond it, seeking the connection that allowed the energy to flow into and out of him. Somewhere during the search, he found the path of the energy streaming to the other dimension, more felt than seen.

"Hold my arm," Michael said, extending that appendage. He felt Akio grab his upper arm, as he clasped Akio's. He looked into Akio's eyes. "I hope to see you on the other side."

"Of what?" Akio asked, but then he was blinded by white energy.

Inspector Hirano was surprised to see what looked like a large black shipping container from decades ago, perhaps even before the war, sitting on the ground behind the trees in the park. The dark allowed it to remain hidden, but he was certain that during the daytime it would be easily seen.

If someone came back here.

Eve walked to the door and lifted a latch.

"You keep it unlocked?" he asked, and then checked himself. "Of course not, there is an electronic lock for when you are gone, and Eve controls it."

Eve opened one of the doors and the lights came on inside. She waved. "In we go, please keep the sticky blood off the floor." She put a hand out, stopping Jacqueline. "That means you." She pointed to the left. "You will find some disposable towels over there. Use them or you get to clean the floor."

Jacqueline nodded and Eve let her enter. Eve looked over at Mark. "Hey, you have blood all over your sleeve! What happened?"

Mark looked down. He had cleaned his hands back inside the building when he was helping to get the police through the rubble of the fourth floor, but the blood was still on his shirt. "I ripped someone's heart out."

"Seriously?" Jacqueline grabbed a towel and tossed it to the ground. Then she used two more to move along until she pulled a seat down, pitched a towel onto it, and sat. "How come?"

Mark pulled down the seat next to her. "He was going to tell some people they should shoot you."

"So," Jacqueline clarified, "let me get this straight."

He nodded.

"Someone says to shoot the tall scary wolf-woman."

"Uh-huh," he agreed.

"And you come up and stick your hand..." she continued.

"Clawed hand," he interjected.

"Clawed hand," she amended. "Through his chest and rip out his heart so no one would shoot me?"

"Well, of course," Mark shrugged. "That bullshit isn't going to fly with me."

"That's pretty hot," Jacqueline murmured, her eyes sparkling.

Yuko smiled as the inspector tried to take in the casual carnage the two younger people were discussing. "You have to forgive them, Inspector." He turned to look at her. "About eighteen or so hours ago, they were in the area we called France. There, outside of the somewhat ruined city of Paris they were standing between a couple thousand Wechselbalg and the humans who call it home."

The inspector blinked a couple of times before turning to the pair, who were ignoring everyone except each other. "Them?" Yuko nodded. "Oh." He processed that thought a moment. "That's why they weren't too worried about a bunch of guns and wolves."

"Well," Yuko shook her head, "part of the reason they didn't run was Michael, of course."

"Who?"

"Michael," Yuko told him. "Think Akio, but even more deadly. There isn't any danger he can't get out of."

MICHAEL LOOKING around the whiteness that was the Etheric Dimension. "We aren't fucking getting out of here."

Akio turned in all directions. "I have been here only a few times with Bethany Anne."

Michael grunted and ran a hand over his bald head. "Yes, she makes my travel through the Etheric look like I'm using a tricycle while she drives a Ferrari."

Akio looked over at Michael. "I'm thinking the right term is 'flies a spaceship.'"

Michael blinked. "I think Jacqueline would say, 'Ouch!' Akio."

Akio shrugged. "Okay, what do you really want to do, and how soon can we get out of here?"

"I'm not fooling you?" Michael asked.

Akio shook his head.

"Hmm." Michael shrugged noncommittally. "If I remember correctly, we walk some distance and then we try to get out."

"How well did you do this last time?" Akio asked as Michael turned and started walking.

"Get out?" Michael asked over his shoulder.

"Figure out the distance," Akio corrected. "It is obvious you got out."

"Well," Michael said and stopped walking, "I figured out the horizontal distance very well, thank you." He waited until Akio was close enough that he could grab his arm. "It was the vertical that was the challenge."

The two men disappeared once more.

JAPAN

THE CONTAINER SET down in a darkened area near the inspector's apartment building, and Yuko opened the door. The inspector walked through and she followed him out.

"What happens now?" he asked her.

She looked up to the stars. "We are moving into our next stage, now that Michael has returned.

"Next stage?"

"Yes." She returned her gaze to him. "We have been in our first phase up until now."

"Where was he?"

"Dead," she replied.

He missed the slight grin on her face. "Dead?" he asked.

She winked. "Not really, just in another location."

"Oh," he murmured, not really wanting to travel too far down a path with a vampire at the end. "May I know what the first phase was?"

Yuko thought about it. "Okay." She waved across the valley and up towards the lights on the mountain. "We were charged by Bethany Anne..."

"Who?" he interrupted. "Sorry," he said when she looked at him.

"She is my Queen, and responsible for Japan being in its current position. So much more advanced than the rest of the world."

"Why did she do it?"

"For Michael," Yuko said. "I did it for her, Akio and Eve both did it for her. Now that we have him, we will be using the preparations we have made here in Japan and elsewhere to finish our job."

"May I ask..." he started.

Only to have Yuko finish for him. "What that job is?"

He nodded.

"We have to make sure the two of them reunite."

"Where is she?"

Yuko held a hand up to the stars, but then pulled it back down a moment later and looked where she had been indicating. "Actually, over there," she said, pointing to another area of the sky.

"She's part of the people that left?" he asked, amazed, and then looked down at her. "You are part of that group?"

"Yes," Yuko said. "That is why we have the technology that helped keep Japan safe through these dark ages."

"And now what are you going to do?" he asked. "Stage two?"

Yuko smiled. "Well, if you care to keep a secret for now?"

He shrugged. "So long as it doesn't include breaking the law."

"No laws, Inspector." She pointed back up. "Now that we have Michael back, we need to build a spaceship so we can all leave Earth."

A few moments later, the inspector told the amazing woman goodbye, not sure if he would see her again, or even remember.

Once the black craft was gone from his sight, he turned and hurried into his building and up to his apartment. Once inside, he grabbed the diary of musings he had written over the years and started describing this evening's events.

The two men stepped out of the Etheric and immediately began to drop. Michael pressed his lips together in annoyance and changed to Myst again as they fell past the top of a ten-story building. He leveled them out and started to head out of the city, then remembered it wouldn't matter. He relocated them to a nearby building that had a solid rooftop. Landing, they rematerialized.

Akio looked around and turned his head slightly. "Eve?" He waited a moment. "Yes, I need the Pod, thank you."

Michael walked over to the edge, his arms behind his back. Akio joined him a moment later. "I wonder how Sabine is doing?" Akio said.

Michael glanced sideways. "How about we check on her in a

few days? We can drop in and read her thoughts, and if she isn't super happy we can have a conversation with her."

Akio nodded his head once sharply in agreement. "I understand," he said to Michael, "about the vertical comment now."

Michael shrugged. "We didn't drown." He turned to the black Pod as it came out of the sky. "And now I have a serious case of wanting to kill him even more."

"Isn't that what Bethany Anne was trying to help you overcome?" Akio asked as the Pod hovered above the rooftop and the canopy came up.

"Hmm," Michael answered as they took off their weapons and laid them in the ship. "Not exactly the killing part, more the *constant* 'kill them all' stick up my ass. I think she did a poor job; her lessons about killing them all didn't stick."

Akio shook his head. "Passing the blame to her is not going to get you points when you two get back together."

Michael jumped into the back seat. "I'll work on my inner peace in the meantime. I figure it's like someone striving to become a vegetarian. There's always the desire to eat meat, if for no other reason than because protein is necessary."

Akio turned to look at Michael. "Have you ever tried to become a vegetarian?"

"Every night from when I go to sleep to when I wake up," Michael replied. "I fall off the wagon usually twice a day. But one day I'll be successful. Then, my goal will be two days in a row."

"So," Akio said as the canopy started to close and the Pod rose, "just plan on trying to be a calm, cool, collected Michael who doesn't kill when he is annoyed every time you go to sleep."

"It's a start, Akio. Don't push it," Michael replied as the canopy locked and the Pod, rising into the sky, turned east.

A pair of eyes watched as the Pod ascended into the sky.

Two Weeks Later

THE MAN DISPLAYED A CROOKED, one-sided smile. "So theoretically if I had, say, a mist, how would I tear apart the atoms of said mist?"

The scientist looked at the aristocratic-looking businessman. "Well, given the energy constraints we have now it might be difficult, at least using any of the more exotic methods we would have employed in the past."

The man tilted his head. "Oh? Why's that?"

The scientist shrugged. "Well, particle physics has relied, for the last couple of centuries at least, on smashing atoms apart and then studying what happened. But in order to accelerate atoms to a high enough velocity to smash them, you need a shit-ton of power. And a certain set of conditions."

The man's brow furrowed at the useless vernacular. "What kind of conditions?"

"Well, a vacuum, for a start," he explained. "Or else all the air molecules get in the way of the atom you're trying to fire at a target to smash."

The man rubbed his chin thoughtfully. "A vacuum, you say?"

The scientist nodded.

He asked another question. "And in order to have a vacuum, you need a sealed chamber?"

The scientist looked at him blankly. "Well, of course."

"So, if air can't get in, then a mist certainly wouldn't be able to get out?"

"That is correct."

The businessman wandered over to the window, deep in thought. "Tell me," he said, barely turning his head in the scientist's direction, "do you have any idea where we might find such a chamber?"

The scientist breathed in. "Well, there were many of them around, once upon a time. The trouble is, most of our research facilities were either destroyed or have since been torn up for parts." The scientist slumped down in the chair, dropping his head into a hand.

The Duke turned to look at him. He could sense a *but* coming.

The scientist looked up. "I suspect there is still a section of pipe in Geneva that might be uncompromised. There was a battle there and half of it was destroyed, but a segment remains. I had been hoping to get back there at some point and see if there was anything there worth experimenting with for fuel cells."

The businessman's eyes glinted. "So, with a vacuum, we could trap a mist for... how long?"

"A mist?" The scientist thought for a moment. "Potentially indefinitely. But it wouldn't be in a vacuum by the time we got it into the tube. Creating a vacuum would take a lot of energy."

"Right, so then tearing apart the mist, once it's trapped? How might that work?"

The scientist's eyes lit and the pace of his speech quickened. "Any number of ways. I mean, if we had power that is. We could blast it with x-ray radiation, or bombard it with gamma rays. There is, well, *was*, lots of equipment there that would allow us to do that. And if the mist were already sealed in a section of tube, that would make things easier and we could do it rather quickly."

The Duke paid close attention to the methods the scientist was reeling off.

"And what if time weren't an issue? Imagine we had decades to wait, or to build..." He led the scientist to continue thinking aloud.

"Oh, well in that case, if rebuilding the accelerator were a possibility..." The scientist's voice trailed off. He paused.

"Hang on. What kind of mist are we talking about?" he asked the businessman, scratching his head with a pencil. "Because there are any number of ways to tear molecules apart, especially with time and energy."

Duke smiled. "Well, that is good to know," he said. "You're hired."

The scientist looked confused. "For what, Mr. Renaud? I didn't apply for anything."

Mr. Renaud's smile disappeared. "You didn't. But you are. Do we have a problem?" His eyes glared red.

The scientist gulped and shook his head.

William Renaud's eyes returned to normal and his face relaxed to its normal resting position. "Good. You start tomorrow. Put your affairs in order. I'll meet you back here. We'll be leaving for Geneva."

He started to leave the man's office before turning back. "You may call me Duke Renaud or, of course, Your Grace."

FINIS

AUTHOR NOTES - MICHAEL ANDERLE

WRITTEN MAY 24TH, 2017

First, let me say THANK YOU that not only did you read this book all the way through, but that you are ALSO reading these notes as well!

This book, The Darkest Night, is WAY overdue. It should have been released about three weeks ago (I was doing about a five-week release schedule before all of the extra series came in) and now, I'm just about at eight weeks. So, I dropped three weeks behinder-er.

On Facebook, I have been HEARING (ok, *reading*) the grief.

However, considering how hard, and the stress it caused, to get this book out this time, I'm not allowing myself a break as I move into FOREVER DEFEND (TKG 17). I already have over 2k words written (which is a record, I think. I'm not sure I have had ANY words for the next book written when the last book wasn't even out, yet.) So, I'm writing these author notes, then I'm going to write some more on that book and see where I get.

A HUGE THANK YOU goes to one of my collaborators, Ell Leigh Clarke (with an 'E') who constantly refers to me as a shriveled up green guy with lots of folds for skin. Now, she deserves lots of kudos (calling me Yoda is not one of them) but specifically I want to say *Thank You* for the last scene of this book.

I was struggling with coming up with scientific ways to… uhhh… truly kill Michael and I learned something. I learned you never ask a physicist (yes, she is one) just how to kill something at the atomic level. It's pretty damned scary when they understand the atoms, the molecular bonds and just how you would go about doing it.

Why Hollywood doesn't talk with more physicists and make them scary bad guys, I don't understand.

She was kind enough to work me through the multiple creative ways to kill Michael, how it could be done in a post-apocalyptic world, and the necessary requirements for making it happen. Then, she was kind enough to just write up the explanation with the physicist and the Duke and put in all of that science-y stuff.

So, *thank you Ellie!*

Speaking of Author Ell Leigh Clarke, her new space opera set in the Kurtherian Gambit Universe is selling *very* well. **THANK YOU ALL** who have read it!

Her first book link is at the end of these notes.

BUSINESS STUFF UPDATE

For those who are following the business aspects of these books, let me give a small update. For the last six months, the ratio of Kindle Unlimited income vs. book sale income is 60/40 (+/- maybe 1-2% max). Which, since generally I make more from a purchased book, means that my Kindle Unlimited has more books read than purchased books. Since Amazon really doesn't give us a breakout, the best I can do is guestimate on some of these items.

Either way, THANK YOU for either reading through Kindle Unlimited, or purchasing the books! Every one of you make this wonderful profession a reality for me and I can't be more blessed.

AUDIBLE

We should have the first month where our outgoing cost(s) to produce Audio is just about in-line with our income from the Audio. To date, we have done 18 audiobooks (3 are waiting for ACX Approval, including book #6 for Bethany Anne.) For the foreseeable future, we will be net-negative with audiobook investment vs. income. I *hope* that we will turn the corner by fourth quarter this year. The reason we won't before then is because our book releases are increasing and therefore we are increasing the quantity of talent we are finding/hiring to produce the audio and so the expenses are ramping up much quicker than the income. The main moneymaker from Audible is The Kurtherian Gambit series (not a big surprise). So, one main income producer that is the one that pays for the rest to be done. The other series look like they will take about eighteen months for most of them to turn profitable.

Which, frankly kind of bites, but that's audio for you.

It's way more money to produce, and not nearly the payback you get with ebooks. The only thing more expensive and less income producing (from what I've heard) is trying to produce and sell translations.

Yeah, I'm not going to go there. However, I am going to go to Frankfurt Book Fair in October (http://www.buchmesse.de/en/fbf/) to try and speak with both traditional publishers (get into bookstores, there is still money to be made there) and to find potential licensing options for foreign markets (outside of English).

KINDLE/KOBO and the Military
So, I have provided a bunch of Kindles to the military (Center for the Intrepid, Fort Sam Houston) and I'm excited about the next option I'm working with KOBO. They have a new device which is waterproof and seems like it would be a fantastic potential tool for our military readers. Further, I know the KOBO representative well enough to know that he will "hook us up" with additional ways for the military contacts to download books

as well. I'm new to the opportunity, (I'm expecting to speak with him today or tomorrow) and see what we can do.

I'm not against Kindles, but if we can get an awesome reader they can dunk in water... I think that's pretty cool!

We will see what happens.

THE REST (just a little sappy)

I just want to thank all of the Kurtherian Fans from whatever method you first picked up one of these books. The change in my life, my family's life, and those that have been helped due to your support has been nothing short of amazing.

From our first efforts chatting with each other on Amazon's forums and Facebook, to all of the ways we communicate now I wish I could just 'tell' every struggling author to get them up to speed.

As some of you know, I'm now considered a 'special unicorn' (shorthand for "don't you expect to be able to do what Michael has") in the community. For those who are happy believing that statement because it relieves them of believing in themselves, so be it.

For the rest, may they aspire to accomplish the EXACT same thing that Kurtherian Fans, readers, and our authors have accomplished. Because (in my opinion) it transcends just authors and readers, it's a group that lives and thrives as a tribe that accomplishes so much more than any of us accomplish alone.

BECAUSE OF YOU, there is a 20Booksto50k group for Indie Authors that has changed lives that is over 9,000 strong. There is also a 20Booksto50k conference (very cheap, no profit involved) to bring indie authors together in Vegas this year, and London next.

Craig Martelle is the man behind that, not me.

Eventually, I'd love to make it to a fan conference, and just get to meet the amazing people behind the force known as The Pitchforks and Matches crowd.

Because, when I've needed a push, you guys and girls provide it.

(Whether I WANTED the push, or not!)

THANK YOU ALL!

Michael

* From earlier in the notes:

Ell Leigh Clarke's first book is here (http://books2read.com/Awakened) and her third book will be out by a week from Monday.

Michael Anderle Social

Website:
http://kurtherianbooks.com/
Email List:
http://kurtherianbooks.com/email-list/
Facebook Here:
https://facebook.com/TheKurtherianGambitBooks/

Stories by Michael Anderle

Kurtherian Gambit Series Titles Include:

First Arc

Death Becomes Her (01) - Queen Bitch (02) - Love Lost (03) -
Bite This (04)
Never Forsaken (05) - Under My Heel (06) - Kneel Or Die (07)

Second Arc

We Will Build (08) - It's Hell To Choose (09) - Release The Dogs
of War (10)
Sued For Peace (11) - We Have Contact (12) - My Ride is a
Bitch (13)
Don't Cross This Line (14)

Third Arc (2017)

Never Submit (15) - Never Surrender (16) - Forever
Defend (17)
Might Makes Right (18) - Ahead Full (19) - Capture Death (20)
Life Goes On (21)

The Second Dark Ages

The Dark Messiah (01)
The Darkest Night (02)

The Boris Chronicles
* With Paul C. Middleton *

Evacuation
Retaliation
Revelation
Restitution 2017

Reclaiming Honor
* With JUSTIN SLOAN *

Justice Is Calling (01)
Claimed By Honor (02)
Judgement Has Fallen (03)
Angel of Reckoning (04)
Born Into Flames (05)
Defending The Lost (06)

The Etheric Academy
* With TS PAUL *

ALPHA CLASS (01)
ALPHA CLASS - Engineering (02)
ALPHA CLASS (03) Coming soon

Terry Henry "TH" Walton Chronicles
* With CRAIG MARTELLE *

Nomad Found (01)
Nomad Redeemed (02)
Nomad Unleashed (03)
Nomad Supreme (04)
Nomad's Fury (05)
Nomad's Justice (06)
Nomad Avenged (07)
Nomad Mortis (08)
Nomad's Force (09)

Trials and Tribulations
* With Natalie Grey *

Risk Be Damned (01)
Damned to Hell (02)
Hell's Worst Nightmare (03) coming soon

The Ascension Myth
* With Ell Leigh Clarke *

Awakened (01)
Activated (02)
Called (03)
Sanctioned (04)
Rebirth (05)

The Age of Magic

The Rise of Magic
* With CM Raymond / LE Barbant *

Restriction (01)
Reawakening (02)
Rebellion (03)
Revolution (04)

The Hidden Magic Chronicles
* With Justin Sloan *

Shades of Light (01)
Shades of Dark (02)

Storms of Magic

With PT Hylton

Storms Raiders (01)
Storm Callers (02)

Tales of the Feisty Druid
With Candy Crum

The Arcadian Druid (01)

<u>The Revelations of Oriceran</u>

The Leira Chronicles
With Martha Carr

Quest for Magic (0)
Waking Magic (1)

SHORT STORIES

Frank Kurns Stories of the Unknownworld 01 (7.5)
You Don't Touch John's Cousin

Frank Kurns Stories of the Unknownworld 02 (9.5)
Bitch's Night Out

Bellatrix: Frank Kurns Stories of the Unknownworld
03 (13.25)
With Natalie Grey

AudioBooks

Available at Audible.com and iTunes

The Kurtherian Gambit

Death Becomes Her - Available Now
Queen Bitch – Available Now
Love Lost – Available Now
Bite This - Available Now
Never Forsaken - Available Now
Under My Heel - Available Now
Kneel or Die - Available Now

Reclaiming Honor Series

Justice Is Calling
Claimed By Honor
Judgment Has Fallen
Angel of Reckoning

Terry Henry "TH" Walton Chronicles

Nomad Found
Nomad Redeemed
Nomad Unleashed
Nomad Supreme
Nomad's Fury

The Etheric Academy

Alpha Class
Alpha Class 2

Anthologies

Glimpse